KIPLING PARK

by

New York Times Bestselling Author

JOE HILLEY

Dunlavy + Gray
HOUSTON

KIPLING PARK

Dunlavy + Gray ©2023 by Joe Hilley

Library of Congress Control Number: 2023933308

ISBN: 979-8-9868156-2-6

E-Book ISBN: 979-8-9868156-3-3

This book is a work of fiction. Names, characters, businesses, organizations, places, events, and incidents either are the product of the author's imagination or are used fictitiously. Any resemblance to any person, living or dead, is coincidental.

Cover design and typesetting by Fitz & Hill Creative Studio.

First Printing, 2023
Printed in the United States of America

"Love your neighbor as yourself."
—Jesus

CHAPTER 1

The coffee was bitter that morning. I don't know why. I made it the same way every day, but that day it was bitter. My uncle told me once that a pinch of salt helped. I had never tried it before, so that morning I did. It didn't work, but rather than pour out the whole potful and start over, I persevered, pouring and sipping my way toward the bottom of the urn as I sat at the dining table.

On the table were maps, plats, surveys, and engineering reports for a real estate development my ex-husband Walt and I were building on the north side of the city. Though I divorced him five years earlier, I retained an interest in the real estate firm we'd spent our careers establishing. I put as much effort into the company as he did, and I wasn't about to lose it. Especially not to a long-legged, large-breasted assistant a third my age.

Hardly a day went by that I didn't think about what happened between us. The life I thought we built through laughter and pain, sacrifice and success. The dreams we had shared, the plans we had made, and the disappointments we'd endured. Just the two of us. We never had children, and now, looking back, I suppose that was for the better, though I never got over it. In the same way I hadn't gotten over finding him naked in our bed with the assistant. And then to learn it had been going on between them for a long time.

With the memory came a deep and abiding sadness. Not the nostalgic sorrow of what had been but never could be again, and not the longing for what might have been but never would be. Rather, an inexplicable aching in my soul that seemed to sink into my bones without relief. Cold, dark heaviness pressing down on top of me, pushing me against the chair bottom, as if to press me into the floor. My arms, too heavy to lift. My legs, too weary to move. So, I sat there and let it push me farther and farther inside myself until it seemed as if I might disappear.

After a while, I realized I was staring blankly ahead. My eyes were focused on the wall at the opposite end of the dining room but noticed nothing. My mind raced at a hundred thoughts per second but failed to settle on any single one. I don't know how long I had been that way but the cup from which I'd been drinking was empty and the light that earlier played across the table had changed from the soft, muted hues of sunrise to the stark glare of a clear morning sky.

A second pot of coffee, much better than the first, took me to mid-morning. By then, my eyes were tired—I had been up since four and was still in my pajamas and housecoat. Rather than pushing through to noon with the tasks at the dining table, I showered and changed clothes, then walked over to my neighbor Phyllis' house. She lived next door with only a driveway and a small patch of grass separating us.

Phyllis and I had known each other since she moved to the neighborhood thirty years earlier. Her husband, Clark, had enjoyed a successful career as an attorney working with some of the city's wealthiest businessmen, most of whom made their money in oil. Phyllis and Clark could have lived anywhere, but they chose Kipling Park. She said it was a good place to raise a family, though their children were almost grown when they moved next door. Clark said they bought it for the price. "You can get more here for the dollar than you can anywhere else in Houston." He saw housing as a commodity. A roof. Walls. Shade from the blistering sun. A building lot for a teardown after the structure lost all its value. He was right back then. Our neighborhood was the best value in Houston. Now, you'd have to go quite a bit farther from town to find a bargain.

When we moved to the neighborhood, Walt said he favored the location because it was convenient for visiting our parents—mine lived in Austin, his in San Antonio. From the beginning, I preferred to work from home. Our quiet street was far more conducive to creativity than the erratic atmosphere of the office. I thought Walt was being kind and supportive in agreeing to let me work that way. After I discovered he was bedding the assistant, I realized he wanted me on the west side because it was too far from the office to conveniently drop in unannounced.

Phyllis was in the kitchen when I knocked on her back door. I could see her through the window. She came to the door drying her hands on a towel. "Why do you always knock?" she asked as she let me inside.

"My mother said it was the polite thing to do," I replied.

"Your mother is long gone."

"Not really," I responded. "She lives right here." I tapped my head for emphasis as I followed her to the kitchen.

"Have a seat," she said, pointing to the table. I sat in the chair on the side near the sink and watched while she poured coffee into a white cup, then set it at my place. Her coffee was always much better than mine. I never refused it, no matter how much I'd had before I arrived.

"Are you going to the party?" Phyllis asked. She smiled at me as she settled into her chair. "I hear all the best from the neighborhood will be there." Her voice had a mocking accent, which caused us both to laugh.

That phrase, all the best, was a thing between us. Someone made that comment a few years ago at another party. We thought it trite and silly, but it quickly found its way into our conversations, usually in things like, "Want to have lunch at Christie's? I hear all the best will be there." To which we giggled like schoolgirls.

"I suppose I'll go," I said slowly. "Not much else to do. But it seems silly. After all, it is February. Silly for the committee to have it now."

"Yes," Phyllis said. "It's February. But it's also Texas. They say the high that day will be eighty-five."

"If the weather follows the app on your phone."

"You know this wasn't the committee's idea. It was all Allison."

"She can't help herself," I said. "Takes advantage of every opportunity to organize something. Tennis club, book club, movie night."

"What was it this time?"

"Valentine's Day is coming."

"Oh." Phyllis nodded. "I forgot about that."

"I don't think that's the theme for it, but that's what got her started on it. I think it's great she wanted to get us all together."

"It is great," Phyllis replied. "Especially since it means I don't have to do any of the preparation."

We giggled again. I took another sip of coffee. "But," I said, "sometimes it is a little too much."

"Well," Phyllis said, "she's good at it and she does seem to enjoy it. Makes it our duty to let her do it."

We laughed again, then I felt a disapproving frown crease my forehead. "But outdoors in February?"

"Relax. It'll be like a spring evening."

"Maybe."

Phyllis glanced in my direction. She must have noticed the cloud descending over me again. "You're in a mood this morning. Have you been brooding over the leggy young assistant again?"

My eyes focused on my cup. "Every time I work on that project, she's there. Or on anything else, for that matter. She's always there. In my mind. Filling my imagination."

"Well," Phyllis said, "I suppose you could always catch her on the way to her car one night and settle things in the parking lot."

We laughed but I didn't want to talk about that topic anymore. "Are we supposed to bring anything to this party?" I asked.

Phyllis shook her head. "I think Allison has it all under control."

Allison Andrews, to whom we referred, lived directly across the street from me. She was about our age, but twice as active. Tennis club, swim club, Christmas committee, book committee, neighborhood movie night. She loved to talk and visit and look after people. Keep them organized. Everyone participating. Everyone happy, by her definition. David, her husband, thankfully, wasn't quite so involved or so energetic. I'm not sure we could stand two like her.

After a moment I could see from the look in her eye that Phyllis was thinking of something else to say. Rather than have her steer our conversation back to Walt's assistant, I said, "Will Bob be there?"

Bob Carter lived up the street in the next block. He was a widower. A little younger. Still with a hint of muscle and angle. He jogged past my house one morning without a shirt.

I watched him to his drive even though I had to move to the far end of the window to do it.

Phyllis looked away. "I think so."

"He likes you."

"Hush."

"Well, he does. You know he does."

"I'm not interested in a man." Phyllis' tone softened. "But I don't seem to be able to convince him of that."

A smile turned up the corners of my mouth. We both knew she wasn't being honest. "Maybe you aren't trying hard enough," I suggested.

She looked over at me. "What does that mean?"

The outside of my cup was damp from coffee that had drizzled down the side. I set it on a napkin to avoid leaving a ring on the table. "I saw him leaving your house the other night."

"We have dinner together sometimes," she responded. "So what?"

"It was after midnight."

She gave a dismissive gesture. "It was nothing."

"Really?"

"We fell asleep watching a movie. That's all."

"And anyone who believes that needs to see me about a house." I stood and moved to the counter to refill my cup.

"Oh, stop." Phyllis sighed. "We're too old to be carrying on like that." But I could tell her heart wasn't in the comment.

"Maybe." I filled the cup, then added sugar. "No one knows how old you really are." She was obsessive about not revealing her age. "Maybe you're not too old for it."

"Well, I'm too old for that, I can tell you for a fact."

We exchanged a look and I realized there was more to it. "Oh," I said. "You mean you actually… You know… tried?"

She looked irritated. "Where does your mind take you?"

Phyllis did her best to sound indignant, but I knew she was only putting on a show to hide the truth. I returned to my chair and looked over at her. "You went to bed with him?" My voice was a whisper. "With Bob Carter?"

Phyllis didn't respond immediately, and I thought I might have offended her. Finally, she said, "I had no idea that sort of thing was even possible now. After so long."

That she might have been romantically involved with someone didn't surprise me. She was attractive enough. Surely, she'd had the chance for it since Clark died. At least the chance to think about it.

I often wondered what it might be like to be with someone. I had never been that way with anyone other than Walt… Well… There was a boy in college in my sophomore year. Handsome guy with broad shoulders and a muscular chest. But only that once. I was so scared we'd messed things up. And more recently there had been Jim Neuhaus, though he didn't count because we didn't do anything like that. Just dinner and a movie a few times, before I broke it off with him. Not even as much as falling asleep together while watching a movie. I knew more than that had transpired between Phyllis and Bob.

Not that being attracted to someone was wrong. Even after the assistant and the divorce and the anger that lingered from it, I still occasionally thought about being with someone. I was genuinely attracted to Jim, but I couldn't bring myself to do anything about it, to press through the hurt to find something new in a relationship, which is why it ended, mostly.

But to be with someone—naked and groping, bare flesh against bare flesh, without being married… The rules that applied when we were twenty still applied when we were sixty. Or, in my case, a little older. Romance, yes. Sex, not outside the traditional boundaries. I couldn't say all of that to Phyllis. Not yet. Boundaries were the result of a perspective. The product, not the ultimate goal. Imposing boundaries without transforming her perspective would have sounded like criticism. Not the way to win anyone to anything except rejection.

People in my Sunday school class might have condemned me for my responses that morning, and for my approach to Phyllis in general, insisting I should have pointed out the evils of a physical relationship outside marriage, but Phyllis didn't attend church and as far as I could tell, she had never made a place of any kind in her life for God. I wanted to be the means for changing that, but it wouldn't be possible if I preached to her. Coaxing was the better option. And for that to occur, we had to relate. I liked that approach and besides which, my life wasn't perfect either.

"It's not exactly the same now as when we were young," Phyllis said, continuing our conversation. "But it is interesting. I suppose. Interesting enough."

I smiled. "At our age, it doesn't take much to be interesting."

We giggled at each other in response.

CHAPTER 2

As the sun was setting on Thursday evening, people from the neighborhood gathered at Allison's house for the neighborhood party. Torches lined the driveway leading from the street to a place near the garage where Allison's husband, David, and several others tended gas grills on which they cooked chicken and sausages. The aroma was interesting, but I disliked sausage and the smell of it brought back memories I preferred to avoid.

Most of the crowd loitered near the swimming pool and under a giant oak tree that stood near the corner of the back yard. A sound system played music through speakers mounted at the corners of the house. I recognized the song that was playing when I arrived. It was popular when I was in college.

Jim Neuhaus was standing at the opposite end of the pool from me, talking to a couple who'd recently moved to the neighborhood from Australia. Something inside me leaped at the sight of him. I hadn't expected him to be there. When he noticed me, he excused himself from the others and started in my direction. Before he reached me, Allison came to my side, gestured to him with a nod, and whispered, "I invited him especially for you."

"For me?"

"You really don't want him to get away." She knew we had been seeing each other before and that I had pushed him away.

"Did you tell him that's why you invited him?" I asked.

"Of course not." She laughed and touched my elbow. "He likes you and you like him. And you know it. So, relax. You could use the company."

Allison was like that. Always with an eye for who needed what and how and when and with whom. She had enjoyed a wonderful first marriage, followed by a romantic second one with an old flame from high school. Classic tale—both single again, but still with plenty of energy, found each other at a high school reunion, and the spark was still there. And having found bliss a second time, she was determined to give us all the same experience. She tried matching Phyllis with a guy from her bridge club, but Phyllis promptly shut her down. I hadn't been so direct with her, partly because I liked her and didn't want to be rude to her, and because somewhere inside I secretly hoped that she could do for me what she'd done for herself in finding life again. And I liked Jim.

Allison moved away. Jim smiled as he came near. "Good to see you, Maureen."

"How are you, Jim?"

"Nice evening for a gathering," he noted. "Couldn't do this in New York right now."

Jim spent his professional career in New York where he worked for an advertising agency. He retired early and moved to Houston with his wife to be near their son. It had been a pleasant arrangement at first, but then Jim's wife died, and his son moved to New Orleans. Adjusting to all of that had been difficult but he seemed to be managing, from what little I saw of him. We had been out a few times—dinner, a movie, an afternoon at the art museum—but my mind was stuck on Walt and the assistant, and the affair that followed, which made it difficult for me to fully invest in a relationship with anyone. After a while, I stopped saying yes to Jim's invitations and he stopped asking. He lived one street over which meant we didn't see each other in the normal course of our daily lives. That was the reason Allison invited him to the party that night. "It's quite pleasant," I said, unsure what else to say.

He gestured over his shoulder toward the driveway where the men were cooking on the grills. "Those sausages smell good. Are you eating?"

I shook my head. "I'm not hungry."

Smoke rose from the driveway and filled the air with an aroma more enticing than the one I smelled when I arrived, but I didn't want anything dripping on my clothes. Chicken of almost any kind was impossible to eat on a paper plate, and sausages were always a mess. Unless I could sit at a table and eat from a real plate with a real fork and knife, and with a real napkin handy, I wasn't interested.

That might have been the end of my conversation with him that night, but for some reason, I found myself unwilling to let the moment pass. "That couple you were talking to," I said before he could step away. "What are their names?"

"Sheila and Gib LaRue," he replied.

"They're from Australia?"

"Yes. He works for one of the oil companies. I don't remember which one."

I faked a disapproving expression. "Another engineer?" The city was full of them.

He laughed. "I think so. Why do you ask?"

"Just curious." I couldn't very well tell him I'd only asked about them to keep him from disappearing.

"You know how it is," he continued. "The oil industry attracts people from everywhere." He smiled pleasantly. Jim had a nice smile. "You should be pleased."

"Why is that?"

"They buy those houses you build."

For some reason, the comment caught me off guard and felt like an intrusion. As if the real estate business I owned with my ex-husband was a private domain. An intimate domain. No one else was allowed. I didn't like the feeling—of him intruding, or of me regarding the business as a private space. I pushed the thought aside and said, "Then may we have more engineers, and may they buy more houses."

He gestured to a table where glasses and cups were arranged next to bottles of beer, wine, and soft drinks on ice in a cooler. "Would you like something to drink?"

I was thirsty and empty-handed—no one should ever be empty-handed at a party—so I said, "Sure," and followed him to the table. He had a beer. I took a glass of wine.

When we had our drinks, we drifted toward the opposite side of the pool, near the oak tree. The ground was uneven, and I took hold of Jim's arm to steady myself. His bicep felt smooth and hard against the palm of my hand. I was surprised by the sensation that ran through my body at the touch of it. He seemed to like it, too, because when I tried to take back my hand, he pressed his arm against his side. Having him next to me was pleasant so I held onto him for the remainder of the evening.

Phyllis was there with Bob Carter. I saw them earlier, before Jim arrived, but avoided them at first, thinking I might like to spend my time that evening with neighbors I didn't see frequently. After I met up with Jim, I got lost in the sound of his voice and paid no attention to anyone else. Eventually, Phyllis and Bob drifted over to us. Bob and Jim were friends. Conversation between the four of us was pleasant and easy. Even then, I did not let go of Jim's arm but remained at his side the entire time. Never before had I become so completely absorbed by him. It felt good, yet strange at the same time and I wondered where those emotions would take me.

A little before nine, people began to drift away. Jim and

I lingered with Phyllis and Bob in the space near the tree as the crowd thinned, neither of us in a hurry to leave. Finally, someone mentioned we should help clean up. I knew Allison had hired a maid service to do that and felt no obligation to help.

We made our way around the pool to the driveway and walked toward the street. I don't remember what we said, only that my mind was preoccupied with wondering what would happen when we reached the curb. Would he say goodnight, or would he see me all the way home? When we reached the end of the driveway, Phyllis and Bob turned toward her house. I tried to move my hand away from Jim, but he said, "I'll walk with you to your door."

My heart skipped a beat, but I was obliged by custom and the memory of my mother's admonitions to demur. "You don't have to do that," I replied, hoping all the while, knowing all the while, that he would insist.

"It's no trouble," he said, and we started toward my house.

As we crossed the street, I racked my brain for something else to say, just to hear his response. All I could think of was, "Would you like to come in for a moment?" To which I quickly added. "I often have hot tea at night. We could have a cup together."

"That would be wonderful," he replied.

"Or, we could have coffee, if you prefer."

"Whichever you like best," he said.

The door was locked. It took me a moment to find the key and get it open. Once inside, I led the way through the dining room toward the kitchen, thinking we would sit at the table back there, but while I was setting up the coffee maker, I noticed Jim wasn't present. I found him at the dining table staring at a surveyor's plat. The sense of intrusion I'd felt earlier returned and I quickly scanned the table to see if anything else had been moved. As far as I could tell, everything was right where I'd left it that morning. Still, it bothered me to have him looking at my papers.

"Let's sit back here." I gestured toward the doorway.

"Sorry," he replied. "I saw the plat and got distracted."

Anger erupted inside me. I snatched the plat from him and crudely folded it, as if to shield the contents from view. "You should learn to leave other people's things alone," I snapped. "This is mine. Not his. Not hers. And certainly not yours!" I slapped the document on the table. "This is mine." I tapped the plat with my index finger for emphasis. "And you can't come in here and start going through my life." The voice was mine, but it was rendered almost unrecognizable by the intensity of my anger. I took a deep breath and tried to relax. "I think you should leave now," I said firmly but calmly. "I can't have you going through my things."

"I'll leave," he said. "But I wasn't going through your things. It was lying right there in the open. I didn't even touch it. And anyway, a plat is a public document." When I didn't respond, he turned away, stepped to the door, and was gone.

After Jim left, I stood at the dining table and unfolded the plat, then smoothed it out and refolded it carefully the correct way, straightening the wrinkles as I went. This was my project. It had been our dream. Our pet. Almost like the child we never had. But no matter what Walt or that woman said, and no matter what the names on the documents said, it was mine and they could never take it away from me. Not him. And certainly not her.

The morning after the party, I was seated at the dining room table, sorting through estimates for installing curbs and drainage on the building site. Our investors wanted to move quickly. Walt's assistant had called twice already. I was civil to her, but I didn't like dealing with her and it put me on edge, especially since he had insisted he could handle everything and had avoided my calls.

Not long after the assistant's second call, the front door-bell rang, and I saw Allison standing on my porch. When I opened the door, she pointed her finger at me and stepped toward me, "Why did you do that?" Her forehead was wrinkled in an angry expression, her eyes ablaze with anger.

I leaned backward, holding onto the doorframe for support. "Why did I do what?" I was offended by her outburst. "Don't point your finger at me like that."

She pushed her way past me and came into the house

as far as the main hallway. I closed the door and turned to face her, repeating my question. "What did I do to get you so angry?" I was confounded by her indignant tone and the very idea of her barging into my home like that.

She wheeled around in my direction. "Jim told me what happened." There was a tone of righteous indignation in her voice. "I can't believe you would treat him that way." She wagged her finger at me again. "You should be ashamed."

Her finger in my face, and her sense of moral superiority, flew all over me. I was determined to defend myself. "He had no right meddling in my business," I retorted. My voice was stern and equally as loud as hers.

Allison was undeterred. She looked past me and pointed toward the documents on the table. "Is that what you were so upset about?" She still had that righteous tone. It grated on my nerves, and I was about to respond, but she stepped around me and entered the dining room.

The hair on the back of my neck bristled. "I'd rather—"

"Just look!" she exclaimed. "All this stuff is lying out there in the open, just like he said." She stood by the table, hands on hips, and glared at me. "He didn't plunder through your papers. You brought him inside your house. You led him right past the table. What did you expect?"

My tone was imperious. "Well, I certainly didn't expect him to read anything. Regardless of where it was lying, those documents are none of his business."

"How could he have avoided it?" Her voice rose in volume and pitch. "Everything was right there for anyone to see."

"It's my business," I replied. "No one else's. Mine. Not hers." Rage erupted inside me and came roaring out. "It was my dream," I shouted. "My vision. My idea. Mine! Mine! Mine! She's not getting her hands on it." I knew I was standing in my own house, talking to Allison, but in my mind, all I could see was Walt's assistant with her long shapely legs and her large, perfectly round breasts. "She's trying to take over and I'm not giving her one damn thing! It's all mine!" My heart raced and my body trembled. I paused to take a breath and then I noticed Allison was staring at me with the strangest expression.

"She?" Allison's eyes were wide, and her mouth seemed to hang open, even as she spoke, the words coming despite her slack jaw. "What are you talking about?"

I pointed to the table. "Those documents," I said. "That is my project. No one else's. It is mine."

Allison still appeared dumbfounded. "You said it was your project and not hers. And she wasn't getting her hands on it."

"She's not," I insisted. "And I'm not letting—"

Allison cut me off before I could get going again. "We were talking about Jim Neuhaus. Not a woman." A deep frown appeared on her forehead, drawing her eyebrows toward each other. "Are you talking about Walt's assistant?"

Shame and confusion swept over me. I felt as if a mask

had been ripped off me and Allison had seen the rage that lived in my soul. Rage that until then I had not been fully aware of. But before I could recover enough to speak, she turned to the table and continued. "It was a survey," she said. "Wasn't it? A map?" Her voice was calmer. The tone she had when she was solving a problem.

"A plat," I said, correcting her.

She lifted one edge of the plat from its place on the table. "This thing right here?"

"Yes."

"David says this sort of thing gets recorded at the courthouse and becomes part of the public record."

David. How did he get into the conversation? He was a nice guy, but he had no business opining on my project. The rage returned and my voice was loud again. "Who the hell cares about David's opinion?"

The comment about David seemed to aggravate her but she ignored it. "If there's a public record of ownership, no one can take it away from you without your consent. They can't steal it."

I wasn't in the mood for that discussion, so I said, "Why are you talking to me like this? Whatever happened last night was between me and Jim. It had nothing to do with you."

She faced me squarely, her finger wagging like a schoolteacher again. "I invited Jim to the party last night because I knew you liked him, and I knew you regretted the way things ended between the two of you a few months ago. I was trying to help.”

“No one asked you to help.”

“But you needed my help,” she said. “The only reason he was at that party was that I invited him, and judging from the way you held onto him all night I would say you were very glad to see him.”

“I didn’t hang onto him.”

“I saw you with him,” Allison countered. “And so did everyone else. We saw how you acted toward him.”

“So? What’s that got to do with anything?” I knew the point she was making, I just hoped to deflect her from it. “I can hold onto—”

She ignored my response. “He was my guest,” she said. “So, I called him this morning to see how things went. He told me about the fit you pitched and how you threw him out of your house.” We stood there, staring at each other, but she wasn’t finished. “Why did you treat him like that?” Her voice was calm, but the righteous attitude from before was still there. “Everything was going great. Why did you do that? Do you even know?”

In truth, I didn’t know what came over me with Jim. At least, not for certain. But I didn’t want to get into that with Allison. Instead of responding to her with another outburst, I stepped calmly to the front door and opened it. “I think it’s time for you to leave,” I said.

She straightened to her full height. “You’re throwing me out, too?”

"Leave, Allison." I gestured with my free hand. "I'm not talking to you anymore about this."

CHAPTER 3

After the trouble with Jim and Allison, I kept to myself and didn't visit with anyone, not even Phyllis. She didn't call me, either, which was odd. Normally, if I didn't show up at her back door by ten, she called to find out where I was. A week or two of this went by, with me not contacting her and her not contacting me. Then one afternoon I noticed she was outside, working in a flowerbed near her front porch. It was a sunny day with clear blue skies and the air was warm enough to make one think spring was near. But we had several cool periods yet to endure before flowers could survive outside, which left me curious about what she might be doing in the flowerbed. She was an excellent gardener and fully aware of the erratic nature of Texas weather. So, I walked over to her yard to check on her.

"Are you planting something?" I asked as I approached.

"No," she replied. "Just pulling out some of the dead stuff."

She was on her hands and knees with her head and shoulders wedged behind a large azalea bush that partially obscured her from view. I moved closer to see exactly what she was doing but as I came nearer, she held up her hand to stop me. "I wouldn't come any closer," she warned.

The tone of her voice surprised me. "Why not?" I asked.

"Haven't you been following the news?"

"About what?"

"COVID," she said.

"The coronavirus?"

"Yes," Phyllis said. "They're calling it COVID now. Some kind of government acronym. They say it's everywhere now."

"I read something about it online." Since before Allison's party, the virus had become a global pandemic. New reports about it were unavoidable and even in that short time, it had come to dominate everyone's conversation. Still, no one seemed to think it would affect us. Not in Texas, or Houston, or Kipling Park. Nothing like that had ever bothered us in the past.

"Are you still not watching the news channels?" Phyllis asked.

"Shows on those channels don't give the news," I replied. "They're all politics. And anyway, to watch them you have to buy a cable package with dozens of channels no one ever watches."

"You need to be informed," she responded. "Now more than ever."

"I am informed." She seemed in a mood, and I wanted to

avoid an argument. "Why are you worried about the virus?"

"They say it's deadly. And very contagious."

"One side says that," I noted. "The other side says it's all a hoax." The nature of the virus and the proper response were topics of hot political debate. One didn't need a three-hundred-channel cable subscription to know that.

"I guess we'll all find out the truth soon enough," Phyllis replied. "Bob thinks he has it."

News about Bob caught me off-guard. To that point, the virus had been merely a story circulating through media outlets. No one I knew had it. No one I knew even knew someone who had it. "How sick is he?" I asked.

"Sick," Phyllis said. "According to what he says."

"You haven't seen him?"

"He won't let me near him. I've been to his window but that's as close as he'll let me get."

"To his window?"

"On the front porch," she explained. "We can see each other and hear each other, but we don't have to worry about infection."

"How does he look?"

"Like he's sick."

"Is he able to move around the house and take care of himself?"

"So far," she said.

"So, why does he think he has it?"

"About three days after the party he started having

coughing spells and his throat was sore. Then a few days later his temperature spiked, and he's had high fevers since."

"Can they treat it?"

"They can do things to help people survive," Phyllis said. "But they don't have a drug for it, and they don't have a vaccine."

"I guess that's why some are calling for quarantines." Part of the suggested response had been for us to distance ourselves from each other and quarantine those with confirmed cases.

"His daughter is coming to take him to the doctor," Phyllis continued. "There's a clinic at the hospital that will see him. They can test him for it."

"Do the tests really work?" That had been part of the political debate on the topic, too. One side claimed the tests were accurate. The other side said the tests were rigged to give a result that supported the pandemic hoax.

"If Bob's daughter is with him, won't she get it?"

"I don't know," Phyllis replied. "I suppose she could. But she's rather insistent. I don't think he could stop her even if he tried."

"I've met her once or twice. She can be very insistent." Bob's daughter could be obnoxious about having her way, but it didn't seem like the time to say too much.

"Yes," Phyllis said. "And Bob's more worried about everyone else than he is about himself. But she's coming and he's going to get tested."

"Does anyone else around here have it?"

"Bob was at the party," she said. "He thinks he might have exposed people who were there. I haven't heard of anyone else with it, but I don't know. If the news reports are accurate, many will get it, eventually."

The part about Jim being at Allison's party hit me hard. Jim and I stood next to Bob and Phyllis most of the night at that party. A dozen others were close by. If Bob was contagious then, we might all have been exposed. "Did you tell Allison about him?" I asked.

"Yes." Phyllis crawled from the flowerbed and turned to a sitting position on the grass. "She's worried, as you can imagine."

"I'm sure she is." I was worried, too, but I didn't say that.

Still seated on the grass, Phyllis drew her knees up to her chest and rested her forearms on them. Her countenance changed and she looked up at me. "Allison told me about her conversation with you." Her voice was lower and more somber than before.

I felt betrayed. "Allison Andrews should learn to keep her mouth shut."

It was a harsh comment and Phyllis recoiled from it, physically leaning away. A frown appeared on her forehead, and she said, "Are you having a problem with something?"

"No." I avoided her gaze. "Why do you ask?"

"You were all over Jim at the party, then you threw him out of the house. And—"

Anger made the muscles in my neck tense. "I was not all over Jim at the—"

"I was standing right there, Maureen," she said, cutting me off with a matter-of-fact tone. "I know how you were with him." Obviously, she and Allison had been talking about me behind my back.

"You don't know—"

She interrupted again. "You held onto him like you were high school sweethearts. Then you yelled at him and threw him out of the house because he showed a little interest in the things that matter to you." Her voice had an edge. "When Allison confronted you about it, you yelled at her and threw her out, too. And now you're aggravated with me. What is going on?"

"Nothing's going on," I snapped. "I have neighbors who can't mind their own business, that's all." And I abruptly turned away and walked back to the house.

For three more days, I remained at home and didn't visit anyone, including Phyllis. Nor did I go out, even to the grocery store. My morning coffee was bitter. The house was dark. And I was lonely. But I couldn't endure another round of amateur analysis by Allison and Phyllis. I stayed home. Kept to myself. And avoided them all.

On the fourth day, however, there was a knock at my

back door. Through a windowpane in the top half of the door, I saw Allison waiting for me to answer. She saw me, too, and motioned for me to open the door. Reluctantly, I let her inside.

"What did I do now?" I had a sullenly sarcastic tone.

She ignored my sarcasm and came past me to the kitchen where she glanced around as if analyzing and assessing. "This is not good," she said in a serious voice. A doorway to the right led to the hallway, she walked as far as the opening and glanced around once more. "No," she groaned with a shake of her head. "This is not good at all."

"What's not good?" I asked.

"It's not good for you to be in here like this," she said. "All shut up in the dark with nothing but yourself for company."

She started up the hallway. I followed after her. "You're my counselor now?" I asked. "Nobody asked you to intrude in my life."

"Somebody needs to."

"I can take care of myself."

She looked back at me over her shoulder. "We both know that's not true."

At the front door, she turned right and entered the living room. She flipped a switch by the door and the overhead light came on. We blinked at the glare but when I reached to turn it off, she grabbed my wrist. "Leave it on," she said. Her voice was stern and commanding. Rather than fight about the light, I left it on, even though it was my house.

She moved to the windows and began opening the blinds. "You need light," she said. "Light is therapeutic."

"I need you and Phyllis to leave me alone."

By then I could see she wasn't going to stop until she'd done what she came to do, so I sat on the sofa and resolved to wait her out. When all the blinds were open, she took a seat in a chair across from me. "Tell me what's wrong," she said. It was an order, not a question.

I wasn't about to give her a straight answer. "Nothing's wrong," I said.

"Maureen." She used her parental tone, "This situation with you and Jim didn't happen in a vacuum. And it isn't going to fix itself. I've heard his side of things. Tell me your version."

That aggravated me. She unloaded on me before, as if Jim's side of the story was correct, without even asking for my side. "Nothing happened," I replied. "Except he was minding my business and I didn't like it and I told him so. And I told you so, too."

"Well, something happened." Her countenance brightened. "And whatever it was, it started in the dining room, right?"

"What difference does that make?"

"Come on." She stood. "Show me."

"Show you what?"

"Jim mentioned something about that plat. You and I talked about it the other day. Show it to me again."

By then, Allison was across the hallway, headed toward the dining room. I came quickly from my place on the sofa and followed her. "No," I said, calling after her. "Don't mess with my things in there." To anyone else, the documents on the dining table would have looked like a pile of rubble, but they were arranged in a way that let me find what I needed. I didn't want her shuffling through them and getting everything out of order.

When I caught up to her, she was standing beside the table. A quick scan of it told me she hadn't touched anything yet. I was relieved.

"So," she said, gesturing. "The trouble began with the plat. I don't see it. Where is it?" I glared at her but didn't respond. After a moment, she picked up a document from the table. "Is this it?"

"Leave that alone!" I shouted, and I snatched the paper from her grasp.

"Is that it?" She pointed to a different stack.

"No, it's not over there," I snarled. The plat lay at the corner of the table, near where I normally sat. I picked it up and thrust it toward her. "Here. This is it."

The document was folded neatly, with the creases all in their original places. She took the document from me and began unfolding it on the table. I grabbed her hand to stop her. "I'll do it," I said, and I slowly unfolded it, being careful not to tear it. When it was fully open, it covered all the other documents that lay on the table.

"What is this for?" she asked.

"If you don't know what it's for, why did you want to see it?"

"This is what you and Jim were fighting about," she said. "I want to know what the problem was. The trouble began with this." She tapped the plat with her finger. "Tell me what this plat means."

"It's nothing."

"It's everything," she replied. "Explain it to me."

I sighed and pointed to the plat. "This is a drawing of a real estate development," I said.

"The one you've been working on with Walt."

"Yes." I had told her about it many times.

"The one you and he dreamed about for the past forty years."

"Thirty," I corrected. "But yes. The one we dreamed about." I felt a lump in my throat, but I choked it back.

"And the one you're determined his assistant won't get."

Whatever emotion I'd felt turned to anger. "It's mine." My voice was a low, guttural growl. "She's not getting one inch of it."

The anger in my voice was unsettling, even to me. Allison was rattled by it, too, but she kept going. "Tell me about the project."

"I've told you about it a thousand times."

"Tell me again," she insisted. "You and Walt started thinking about this a long time ago."

"Walter," I said. "His name is Walter." I don't know why I said that. I called him Walt all the time. No one called him Walter.

"Tell me about the project," Allison repeated.

"We started on this thirty years ago. A neighborhood we could plan and build exactly like we thought it should be. A town. With everything in its best place. Neat. Clean. Efficient. Friendly. We drove all over the county looking for sites. Eventually, we found a place and started putting it together, one piece at a time."

"And then you found Walt in bed with his assistant."

A lump formed in my throat again. I could only nod in response.

She gestured to the plat. "You fought over this project in the divorce?"

I cleaned my throat. "Walt couldn't afford to fight over it. Not in public. And certainly not in court. It would have ruined everything. Might have scared away our investors."

"So, you divided it."

"We split ownership of everything," I explained. "I got half of the money, half of the firm." I gestured to the plat. "And half of this project."

"And here it is," she said. "Spread all over your dining table."

"You say that like it's a bad thing."

Allison looked me in the eye. "I'm going to say something that you probably won't like, but I mean it in the kindest way possible. This project has become your marriage."

"My marriage?" I didn't want to think about it that way, but her words resonated deep inside me.

"An archetype," she said. "A substitute for your marriage."

"I don't—"

"You and Walt were young when you first started thinking of this. Spent hours together talking about it. In the car. At the table." Allison's gaze never left mine. "Talked about it in bed after you had sex. And before you went to sleep. When you got up and while you ate breakfast."

"We were in love," I responded. It was a magical time for us both. Just a couple of kids dreaming dreams we weren't sure would ever come true. Glimpses of those days flashed through my mind and with each one, pain struck deep in my soul. "It was just the two of us. We spent hours and hours on it. Together."

"Now," Allison continued, gesturing with both hands as she spoke, "the love is gone and this room, these documents, this project has become the substitute for the thing that never happened. This room is a shrine. Half of it devoted to your failed marriage and half to your bitterness and anger over the way it ended."

The pain was too deep. I couldn't bear it any longer, but I didn't want to cry. Instead, my eyes narrowed, and I clenched my teeth tightly. "You have no idea what you're talking about," I seethed. I just wanted her to shut up. "No idea at all."

"People only say that when they hear the truth," she said. "Your marriage ended five years ago, yet every day you come in here and think about what might have been and about the girl who stole your husband, forgetting your husband threw you away in exchange for her."

Anger had been building inside me and I wanted to lash out at her, but just as I was about to, the energy drained from my body. The anger evaporated. Only pain and sadness remained. Deep abiding pain. Heavy, debilitating sadness. Tears came to my eyes, but Allison didn't stop.

"When this project was a dream you had with Walt, it was good," she said. "It was right. It brought out the best in you. But now this project has become Walt. It's like, if you can hold onto the project, you can hold onto him and the past and the person you thought you would become."

"It's not bad to hope." My voice was weak, tears trickled down my cheeks, and I seemed on the verge of an emotional collapse. "It's not bad to hope," I repeated in a whisper.

"This project was from a different time," Allison said, "with different people. That time is over. The people who dreamed it up, have moved on. They've gone in separate directions."

"Stop," I sobbed, covering my ears with my hands. "Please stop. I don't want to hear anymore."

Allison's tone softened and she moved my hands away. "You like Jim. I know it and you know it, too. You like Phyllis.

She's your friend. And in spite of yourself, you like me. And I like you." She put her arms around me and hugged me close. "But you can't keep hanging on to Walt and what he did to you. You talk about it in terms of the assistant and what she did, but the person you're really angry at is Walt. And I agree, he treated you like shit. After thirty years, he ditched you for her. But if you don't let that go, it will kill you. It will eat at you and—"

I buried my face in her shoulder. "Walt's getting married," I said.

"Getting married?"

"Yes."

She leaned away and stared at me. "To the assistant?"

"Yes." I pulled free of her grasp and sagged onto a chair at the end of the table. "He called me a month or two ago and told me he was going to ask her. Wanted me to know there would be an announcement in the newspaper." I pulled the article from beneath a stack of papers and handed it to her.

"Oh, Maureen," she said as she scanned it. "I am so sorry."

I wiped my cheeks with my fingertips. "Stephanie, the assistant, is pregnant."

"Stephanie? That's her name?"

"Yes," I replied.

Allison stood beside me and put an arm around my shoulder. "I am so sorry," she repeated.

Tears ran down my cheeks again. "While we were married, he told me it was okay that we didn't have children. Now, he's giving her the baby I was supposed to have." I took a deep breath and let it slowly escape. "Damn his sorry ass." I knew I wasn't supposed to talk that way, or even think that way, but the emotion of the moment was overwhelming.

CHAPTER 4

After Allison's visit, I sat in the dining room and thought about what she had said and about the state of mind I had cultivated over the previous five years. She was right, I had focused my anger on Stephanie rather than on Walt. Probably because it was convenient—Stephanie was much younger and quite attractive, which clashed with my long-held body type issues—but also because it avoided the most painful aspect. He had dumped me. Traded me in for a new one, much the way he traded automobiles or swapped real estate. A transaction. Get rid of this, acquire that. I saw it now. I understood it. I realized what Allison had said was the truth. But it still hurt.

For the remainder of the day, I wallowed in five years' worth of accumulated emotional pain—wrinkles, sagging, softening … rejection—but as sunlight faded from the room, I began to think of how much time I had spent at the dining table. Much of it wasted time, twiddling over endless details already decided and work already settled. Phone calls, questions, emails, texts. Most of it was about things that didn't matter at all. Had I made it all up in my mind as a way of injecting myself into his life? Reminding Stephanie of what she'd done? Reminding him of what he'd done? Hanging on. Holding on. Hoping?

"I might be crazy," I whispered.

Then I remembered Walt's wedding announcement. I read it again and as I did, the finality of the divorce we'd reached five years earlier became real to me in a way it never had before. He was moving on. He had moved on. New wife. New life. New family. New dreams he discussed with someone else in the sexual afterglow.

Strange as it may seem, that was an epochal moment for me—a life-changing turn five years in the making. Everything seemed different. It looked different and smelled different. As I let my eye scan the documents on the table, a sense of morbidity came over me. I remembered sorting through my grandfather's papers after he died. He had been a towering figure in my life. Big and athletic and full of energy. When I rode to town with him, the vitality of his existence enveloped us and energized everyone we met along the way. At lunch in the café, people of every sort crowded around our table, talking and laughing and telling stories. But after he died, and we were at the house going through his things, it all seemed small and stale and of very little significance. As if when he died, everything he'd touched died too. That's how the papers on my dining table, and the project they represented, seemed to me. Dead. Lifeless. Irrelevant. Devoid of meaning. But how could I move on? How could I find whatever was next? And what was next?

Several years earlier, we had a book club at church. It didn't last long but while we were meeting, one of the women in our group mentioned a book by a guy who'd spent a lifetime studying personal relationships. I was intrigued by her enthusiasm for it and purchased a copy. One of the chapters talked about how we sometimes live our way into an emotional cul-de-sac, going round and round and unable to find our way out. The writer offered forgiveness as the key to restoring our lives to their proper path. It sounded trite years earlier when I first read the book, but sitting there at the table, trying to think of what was next, that book came to mind and the topic seemed interesting again. Maybe he was right. Maybe forgiveness was the key.

I retrieved the book from a shelf in the bedroom and skimmed through that chapter. It included exercises designed to apply forgiveness in an empowering way. One of them was to think of everyone you could forgive. Not everyone who merited your forgiveness, but everyone who had ever done anything to trouble you in any way. Regardless of whether anyone else would agree that their conduct was offensive, regardless of whether someone else might be offended if that same conduct was directed at them. If they had troubled you in the least, their name went on the list.

As I read that, a list of people formed in my mind. Possibilities. Maybe. Not that I had decided to actually forgive any of them, but a list of those who had crossed me. People who had hurt me. Made me mad. Walt was the first person who came to mind. And Stephanie. Then more people came to mind and soon a stream of faces and instances. The guy who cut me off in traffic. The one who took a parking space ahead of me. The lady who pushed past me with a shopping cart in the store. Someone who took too long in the drive-thru line. And that idiot with the big-ass pickup truck blowing black exhaust smoke everywhere. The list began to grow.

While I wrestled with the idea of forgiveness and what it might mean for my own situation, I moved from the chair where I'd been sitting and drifted around the table, sifting aimlessly through the documents. Thinking. Remembering. Tears came to my eyes, and I was on the verge of sinking into the darkness that had enveloped me before. Walt. Stephanie. Her perky smile that enraged me. Somehow, I pushed those thoughts aside and came back to the moment, but it was a constant struggle.

Eventually, one or two of the documents caught my eye. Details in them brought to mind events to which they pertained—a meeting, an argument, a decision. Some of the documents related to each other and I put them together, then found more that went with them and added them to the stack. Before long, I forgot about Walt and his lover and turned intentionally to the task of sorting things on the table into stacks according to date and topic. Permits and applications in one spot, soil testing results in another, engineering in a third, working my way around the table as the stacks grew. Afternoon faded to evening. Night fell and the room grew dark, but I was energized like never before.

Many of the documents were things I'd been hoarding. They were outdated and no longer necessary, but I wouldn't let them go. It was apparent to me that they could be stored and never missed. I found an empty file box in the hall closet, brought it to the table, and placed the oldest documents in it. The next oldest followed and the box quickly filled, then I went looking for another. The process continued late into the night—sorting, stacking, boxing.

A little before 3:00 a.m., and for the first time since the divorce, the table was cleared. Its top was shiny and radiant in the glare of the overhead light. Only the plat remained, folded neatly and resting at the place where I normally sat. A thick, oversized document, it had been folded and unfolded many times. The lines and numbers written on it provided a summary of my life with Walt. In a sense, it was the essence of our life together, reduced to its essential detail.

Too tired to go to bed, I took a seat in the chair at the end of the table and unfolded the plat. I spread it flat on the smooth, bare tabletop and stared at it, studying its lines and angles, expecting to recall poignant scenes from my life with Walt. I even tried to steer my mind in that direction, but nothing came. Instead, all I could think was, What a pity that this is all there is. We could have done so much more.

I tried once more to bring back the past and with great

effort succeeded in recalling one or two memories, but they were hollow now. Only echoes from a place where I no longer lived. The life sucked from them by Walt's betrayal.

Finding no peace in the past, I turned my mind to the present. Coffee with Phyllis in the mornings. Allison's party in February. Seeing Jim and holding onto his arm as we stood near the pool. The soothing sound of his voice close to me. The grating shrillness of mine when I yelled at him. When I yelled at Phyllis. And at Allison….

Sometime later I became aware of sunlight streaming in shafts across the room and found I was slumped to one side in my chair at the dining table. The plat was still on the table in front of me. As my eyes focused on it, a sense of hollowness swept over me as it had the night before. It was meaningless to me now, but I could sense it pulling my mind back to the past. The trips we took in getting the project started. Stephanie and her ample chest. Walt noticing her every move. I wanted to—

"Enough!" I shouted. A file box sat on the floor beside the chair. I flipped off the top, snatched the plat from the table, and tossed it into the box, then quickly jammed the top in place. Voices in my head went silent. Peace returned and I was able to think clearly.

Almost immediately I began to wonder if Walt was treating me fairly in our settlement. Was I getting all the income to which I was entitled? Had he padded expenses in his favor? Was he funneling money to Stephanie?

"Quiet!" I shouted.

As an owner of the company, I received monthly income and expense reports from the office bookkeeper and reconciled reports from the tax accountant. I had access to the bank accounts and regularly compared the flow of money against work reflected in records from the office. I could do that as often as I chose. Whatever I had been doing at the dining room table was only my own doing. A trap of my own creation. With it gone, I would be free to do as I pleased. All I had to do was call the office and have someone pick up the boxes.

After a cup of coffee and a shower, I called the office. To my surprise, Stephanie answered the phone. That's when I learned most people were working from home. "We thought it would be safer for everyone that way," she said. "With COVID and all." They made that decision without consulting me. She and Walt. No doubt, it was her idea. Not even officially married to him and already she was running the business. My business. At least half of it.

"The decision has been made," I told myself. "And you can't have it both ways. You're either in, or out." It took me about half a nanosecond to evaluate the situation. I knew the access codes for the building, and I had a key to the office. I could go there anytime I chose, so I thanked Stephanie for her help and ended the call cordially.

When I finished talking to Stephanie, I loaded the boxes in the car and drove them to the office myself. She met me at the door. "There's no one here to help," she said.

I detected a hint of aggravation in her voice but ignored it. A glance at her midriff told me she was farther along with the pregnancy than Walt had suggested. "I just need to put some things in my office," I replied. Nothing was going to deter me from getting those documents out of the house.

After three trips to the car, all the boxes were stacked against the wall in my office. I took a seat behind my desk to catch my breath. While I rested, I checked the mail that had accumulated in my inbox. Most of it was of no importance, but a few things required attention. I bundled them together with a rubber band and took them to Stephanie's office.

"You'll need to take care of these," I said. She had an inbox like mine on her desk, and I dropped the bundle into it. As they fell into place, our eyes met. "We should at least acknowledge each other," I said. It was as close to forgiveness as I could get at the moment.

"I don't want any trouble between us," she said.

"And neither do I."

The moment was surreal. Talking to my ex-husband's lover—who was pregnant with his child—as if she hadn't ruined my life. Two days earlier, I would have slapped her, but right then all I thought about was the book on my shelf from the guy who said forgiveness was the key. I resolved to keep practicing it, however imperfect the form might appear.

"Well," I said, "the documents I had at the house are in my office now. You and Walt can run the project. Let me know if you have any questions."

"Yes, ma'am," she replied.

That flew all over me. Talking to me like I was her elder. And her with my ex-husband's baby growing in her belly. The rage I'd been trying to control flared up inside me, but I wasn't going back to that. Being mad at her had occupied too much of my life already. I took a breath and glared at her. "Don't ever say that to me again."

She seemed startled by my intensity. "Say what?"

"Don't ever call me ma'am."

"Oh. Yes, ma—" She caught herself. "Okay, Maureen."

When I returned home, I parked the car on the driveway at the garage and walked over to Phyllis' back door. If forgiveness was the key to relationships, I needed to apologize for the way I acted that day when she was working in the flowerbed. She was one of my best friends. I couldn't allow trouble to fester between us.

On my way across the yard, I noticed a light was on over the stove in Phyllis' kitchen—I saw it through a side window that faced my driveway. Another was on in the hall, but the remainder of the house was dark, the way a house looks in the daytime when no one's home.

At the back door, I knocked harder than usual, in case she was on the front side of the house, but there was no immediate response. A window to the right of the door afforded a view of the kitchen from the back porch. When no one answered the door, I moved over to it for a look inside, just to make sure, but saw nothing to indicate anyone was present.

I was about to leave when Phyllis appeared at the far end of the hall, near a staircase that led to the second floor. She wore a robe and house slippers and even from a distance I could see she had on no makeup, which was unusual for her. She clutched the robe around her, holding it tightly against her body with both hands, and started toward me.

As she passed through the kitchen, she took a chair from the table and pushed it close to the window, then sat down hard on it. Her lips moved but I couldn't hear a thing she said.

"I can't hear you," I said. "What's wrong?"

She pushed herself up straight in the chair, leaned closer to the window, and spoke louder. "I'm sick," she said. "They tell me I have COVID."

"Were you tested for it?" A test for the virus was available but they still had no drugs to treat it.

"Yes," she said. "At a site in the hospital parking lot."

"What did they do for you?"

"Nothing." She shrugged. "There's nothing they can do."

"What can I do for you?"

"You can't come in here," she said. "This thing is highly contagious."

"But I can't just watch."

"I'm all right for now," she said. "If it gets worse, we could put a box by the door like I did for Bob."

To keep Bob supplied with food, she had placed a Styrofoam cooler by his front door. She put containers of food in it for him. He opened the door after she was gone and got them out.

"How is Bob?" I asked.

"He's okay," she replied. "Not well but holding on."

"Is he in the hospital?"

"He's at home," she said.

"Is anyone checking on him?" She was in no position to help anyone now.

"His daughter checks on him." Phyllis caught my eye. "I heard you talked to Allison."

"I am so sorry for the way I acted toward you the other day. Will you forgive me?"

"Of course."

"I'm sorry."

"It's okay," she said.

"Did she tell you Walt is getting married?"

"Yes," Phyllis replied. "To the assistant. What's her name?"

"Stephanie."

Phyllis nodded. "I think I met her once." She did. At a party we held on our back lawn. I should have known then that something was happening between her and Walt. The looks. The tiny gestures. At the memory of it, a twinge of anger ran through my body. I shrugged it off and repeated to myself a phrase that I was to repeat many times in the future, I forgive them, Lord.

We talked a while longer, but I could see Phyllis was tired and did not look well. "You need to get to bed. Is your cell phone charged?"

"Yes," she replied. "I have a charger down here and one upstairs."

"Good. Keep your phone on."

She smiled in response, and we exchanged a goodbye wave. I waited at the window while she made her way to the stairs, then disappeared.

As I crossed the driveway toward the house, my phone rang. I glanced at the screen and saw the call was from Allison. "You're spying on me," I said with a chuckle.

"You're right there on your driveway," she replied. "You found out about Phyllis?"

"Yes," replied. "Do you have it?"

"No," she said. "Not yet."

I was at the backdoor by then but rather than go inside I sat on a porch chair and continued to talk. "I'm sorry for the things I said when you came to see me last time."

"That's okay," she replied. "It's been a tough situation for you."

"I also wanted to thank you," I continued.

"Thank me. What for?"

"For forcing me to see things the way they are."

"I was just trying to help."

"I know," I said. "And I appreciate it."

"Have you talked to Jim?"

"Not yet. Have you heard from him?"

"No," she replied. "But I'm a little worried about him. He hasn't been at the tennis courts lately. I'm not sure what's going on. We haven't seen him much since the party."

"I'll go over there," I replied. "I need to talk to him anyway."

"Good."

Something in her voice made me think the purpose of her call was to prod me into talking to Jim, but I didn't argue with her about it. Instead, I accepted it as her attempt to help me complete the amends I needed to make with my friends. I needed to talk to Jim and apologize, but the thought of it left me apprehensive.

Of all the people I had offended, Jim was the most personal. If Stephanie had refused to join me in a rapprochement, I wouldn't have thought it any great loss. After all, she'd been sleeping with my husband and was carrying his baby. Phyllis and Allison were important to me, but we had a long history with each other, and this wasn't the first time one or the other of us had offended the other. I knew they would find a way to forgive me and probably already had even before I asked. But Jim … I needed things to be right with him and the on-again, off-again nature of our relationship gave me no confidence things would ever be right again.

When I finished talking to Allison, I walked to the car and drove around the corner to Jim's house. I parked on the street at the curb and followed the walkway to the porch. The house seemed dark and lifeless as I pressed the button for the doorbell. No one came when I pressed it the first time, so I pressed it again, then finally gave up and started back to the car.

As I slid onto the seat behind the steering wheel, my phone rang. I took it from my purse and saw the call was from Jim. "Are you inside?" I asked.

"Upstairs," he said. His voice was little more than a groan.

My heart sank. "Are you sick?"

"I have the virus."

"You sound awful. How do you feel?"

"Worse than I sound."

"Have you eaten anything today?"

"I can't remember," he said. "I've been in the bed since they tested me. I think that was … several days ago. I can't remember when, exactly."

"Is the door locked?"

"Don't come in here," he said. "I don't want you to get sick."

"Is there a key under the mat?"

"No. But seriously, don't come in. You don't want to feel like this."

I wasn't giving up that easily. "Is the back door locked?" I asked.

He sighed. "There's a key in a magnetic box on the control panel for the sprinkler system. But don't—" I ended the call before he finished, came from the car, and started toward the back of the house.

The control panel for the sprinkler was mounted on the wall of the garage. A small metal box was affixed by a magnet to a bracket at the bottom of the panel. I pulled it loose, slid open the top, and found a door key inside.

After opening the door and grappling with the alarm system, I went upstairs where I found Jim buried beneath the covers of his bed in the primary bedroom. "You shouldn't be here," he said.

The room was warm, too warm for me, and it smelled like a gym. "You really haven't eaten?" I asked.

"I don't think so."

"Are you hungry?"

"A little."

"I'll fix you some tea and toast."

I made my way to the kitchen, found the bread and tea, and in a few minutes was back upstairs with a tray. He ate the toast without comment, then sipped the tea and seemed to perk up a little. "I wasn't sure I would ever see you again," he said.

Tears filled my eyes. "I am so sorry for the way I acted and for the things I said. I should have never done that to you."

He smiled. "It's okay. You've been through a lot." The phrase was the same as the one Allison used and I knew right then that they had been talking. She had been running interference for me. Softening the way. Planting in his mind the notion that I had been through a lot with the divorce and all that happened. I bristled at the thought of her interfering, and, at the same moment, gave thanks.

"I could explain some of it," I said, "if you wanted to know, but—"

He held up his hand in a gesture for me to stop. "You don't have to explain anything to me. I have an idea of what you've been through. After my wife died, I left everything downstairs just the way she had it. Somewhere inside, I thought that if I left it that way, she would return. Then one day, my daughter rearranged the furniture in the living room. I was so angry." His eyes glistened. "Started shouting at her." His voice trailed away. "It was awful."

"Did you put things right with her?"

"Eventually," he said. "She understood. I think."

A tear ran down my check. "I never wanted to yell at you or throw you out of the house."

He reached for my hand, then hesitated. "I don't think we're supposed to touch. They say that's one way the virus is spread."

I grabbed his hand in mine. "I can always wash my hand."

"I would kiss you," he said, "but that really would be risky."

We laughed, but I was sorely tempted to kiss him anyway.

CHAPTER 5

The next morning, I returned to Jim's house and made sure he ate breakfast. When he was settled, I went to Phyllis' house to check on her. She failed to respond at the door, so I phoned her, but she didn't answer. She kept a key under a flowerpot in the garden near her back fence. I retrieved it and let myself inside.

"It's me," I said with a loud voice as I came through the kitchen. "Are you upstairs?"

There was no response, so I made my way to the staircase and went up to see if she was there. I found her in bed, conscious but listless and laboring to breathe. As I did with Jim, I prepared toast and tea and took it to her on a tray. She was unable to eat it at first, but I held the toast for her, and she took a few bites, then I held the cup while she took a sip.

"You shouldn't be in here," she said weakly.

"Jim told me the same thing."

"He knows you're here?"

"No," I replied. "But that's what he said when I went to see him."

"He has COVID?" she asked.

"Yes."

"How bad is he?"

"About like you."

"This is the worst I've ever felt." She looked scared and she rested her head against the pillow. "I'm not sure I'm gonna make it."

"I'll help you," I replied. "We'll make it."

"Not if you keep coming in here. You'll get sick too."

"Maybe." I shrugged. "Maybe not. I'm not denying the virus is a threat, but I'm not sitting at home in fear while you're this sick." I helped her take another sip of tea. "You need to drink as much as you can."

"I don't feel like doing anything."

"Are you able to sleep?"

"Some, but it's not restful." Her eyes were full as she looked at me. "I'm afraid if I go to sleep, I'll forget to breathe."

A verse came to mind and before I knew it, I said, "God has not given us a spirit of fear." I don't know why I said that. I've never quoted scripture to people like that and certainly not to Phyllis. But there it was.

"Sounds likc the Bible," she replied.

"It is, but I don't remember which verse."

"Do you think I'm going to die?"

"I think you should concentrate on getting well." I set the teacup aside and straightened the cover. "And repeat that verse in your mind when you feel afraid."

"I'm not sure I believe in God."

"That's okay," I replied. "He believes in you." It sounded cliché, but it was true, and I didn't try to qualify the statement. My mother used to say that sometimes cliché answers were all there were.

Phyllis responded with a smile and closed her eyes. I sat by the bed and read aloud to her until she drifted off to sleep.

With Phyllis asleep, I returned home and had lunch. As I was rinsing my plate at the sink, the phone rang with a call from Allison. "Did I see you coming from Phyllis' house a little while ago?" She could be so nosy at times.

"Yes," I replied.

"She has COVID," Allison said coldly. She was so condescending sometimes.

"I know."

"And you were in there with her?" Her tone and volume rose with every word.

"I made something for her to eat."

"You shouldn't be in there."

She sounded like a schoolteacher scolding a child. I bristled at the sound of it. "I can't just leave her there," I replied.

"You have to," Allison insisted. "It's not safe for you to be in there."

"Since when did safe become our standard?"

"You could get sick," she said. "And the way they talk on television, you easily could die. Which is probably what the liberals want." Allison and David kept the television on all day, tuned to one of those conservative news channels. Their days were saturated with talk show hosts promoting the latest conspiracy theory.

"You should turn off the TV," I said. "Listen to music."

"Are you one of those science deniers they're talking about?"

I wasn't interested in an argument, but I wasn't going to be bullied by her, either. "You and I go to the same church," I replied. "How many times have they told us we are obligated to care for each other?"

"Calling to check on someone is one thing," she said. "But going in the room with a sick person is crazy. Especially someone who is sick with this kind of illness."

"Is that what Jesus said?" I rarely played that card with anyone, but she was getting on my nerves. She didn't respond and there was silence for too long, so I said, "Look, I'm not trying to be rude, but Phyllis is our neighbor. She needs help and there's no one else to help her but us. If those stories they tell at church mean anything, they mean we are supposed to care for each other, regardless."

"I'm not sure that applies right now."

The error in that statement was so obvious and banal, I didn't know what to say. I wanted to reach through the phone and shake her, but I forced myself to remain calm.

A lot had happened between us in the past few weeks, and I didn't want to turn things upside down again. "I know the risks," I said calmly. "I know this is serious. But I'm not turning my back on our friends. Especially not now."

That sounded strange coming from me. Only a few days before, I had shouted and yelled at all of them—I even threw Allison and Jim out of my house—over a piece of paper that lay on my dining room table. But having come away from that, I didn't want to return, either to the bitterness that fueled my rage, or the fractured relationships it produced.

"I'm just trying to help our friend," I said in a conciliatory tone. "You'll have to help me."

"Help you?" She sounded incredulous. "Help you do what?"

"I don't know, but it will take time for Phyllis and Jim to get well and—"

"Jim?" She all but shouted. "You've been over there, too?"

"Sick people need help," I said.

"I'm not going into their houses," she insisted. "And if you've been in there, I don't want you around me, either."

"They need to eat to get better," I said. "You can cook."

"And who's going to take it to them?"

"We'll figure that out as we go."

"There's no figuring anything out," she railed. "I don't want to have anything to do with them."

"If we go down," I said, "we should go down loving our

neighbors as ourselves."

"This is different. It's too risky."

"Look," I said. "All you have to do is—" A beep from my phone interrupted me and I saw that she had ended the call.

In her heart, Allison was a good person. Under normal circumstances, she looked after others and tried to do her best for them. But these weren't normal times. Everyone was stressed by the threat of a global pandemic. Even those who said they weren't bothered by it were bothered by it. Still, an attitude like that, coming from someone I knew well. Someone I sat with regularly in church, who heard the same sermons I heard, now cowering in fear …

"Lord," I whispered. "I forgive her."

After talking to Allison, I made myself a cup of tea and settled into a chair in the bedroom to re-read that book about forgiveness. The whole thing, not just the single chapter. Things were changing with me. I liked it. And I didn't want it to stop. But I didn't want to be arrogant about it, either. Especially not with Allison. After all, she was the person who refused to let me live with bitterness and anger toward Walt and Stephanie.

A few pages into the book, I fell asleep and when I awakened, I found my reading glasses had slipped from my nose and were lying in my lap. The book was on the floor near my feet. Thankfully, the teacup sat on a table to my left, though I didn't remember putting it there.

I retrieved the book from the floor and set it with my

glasses next to the cup with the idea of going to the kitchen for more tea. Before I could get out of the chair, my phone rang. The call was from Allison.

"Not again," I sighed. But she was my friend, so I answered it. "Hello, Allison," I said in a friendly voice. "Seems like we just talked."

"I'm sorry I got so upset," she said. "I'll do whatever I can to help with Phyllis and Jim, but I have some bad news."

Before the pandemic, a statement like that from her could have indicated real trouble, or it could have been merely the lead to something ironically humorous. She had a dry sense of humor. But with all that had happened since February, I wasn't sure what she would say.

"Oh," I replied. "What is it?"

"Bob Carter has died."

The news startled me. "He died?"

"The ambulance is up there now."

Earlier, I had slipped off my shoes. Now I worked my feet into them while I continued to talk. "Does Phyllis know?" I leaned forward to slip the shoes over my heels.

"I don't think so," Allison responded

"Don't tell her," I said.

"She has to know. We can't keep it from her."

"I'll tell her. But let me check on Jim, first."

"You don't believe me?"

"I believe you. But when I tell her, she'll have questions, and I want to be able to answer them.'"

By the time the call ended, I was at my front door. I shoved the phone in my pocket and stepped outside. Bob lived in the next block. I could see his house from my porch, and I glanced in that direction. A firetruck was parked on the street near the end of his walkway with a paramedic truck and an ambulance behind it. I hurried in that direction as quickly as I could without running.

No one was outside the house when I arrived, and the front door was open, so I let myself in. A fireman stopped me in the hall. "You can't be in here," he said.

"What's wrong?" I asked. "Has something happened to Bob?"

The fireman stepped toward me, gesturing with his hands for me to move back. "It's not safe for you to be in here."

"Not safe?" A frown wrinkled my forehead. "Why not?"

Melinda, Bob's daughter, appeared behind him. Her eyes were red and puffy from crying. "Maureen," she sobbed. "Daddy's dead."

She stepped around the fireman, and I hugged her with both arms. I would have stood right there with her, but the fireman insisted we move outside. We walked to the front porch, and she told me, "A couple of days ago he had trouble breathing. I came over to see about him and found out he hadn't been eating. Phyllis had been helping me and I thought she was doing his meals, but I think she's sick now, too."

"Yes," I replied. "She's very ill. I saw her this morning."

Melinda nodded. "I gave Daddy something to eat and thought he was getting better, but last night he was gasping again. I wanted to take him to the hospital, but he refused. He has a CPAP machine and the doctor said that was the best thing, so I helped him get the mask on and he was using it, and everything seemed fine, so I went home." An anguished expression wrinkled the corners of her eyes. "When I came back this morning, he was just lying there in the bed. Not breathing or moving or anything." Her lip quivered.

The front door opened, and the fireman appeared. "We're going to bring him out, now," he said. "Y'all might want to move back from the door."

I guided Melinda to the opposite end of the porch, and we stood together as they brought Bob's body from the house. He was covered with a white sheet and strapped to an ambulance stretcher. I was glad for Melinda's sake they didn't use a body bag. They look so final and awful.

The fireman stood with us until the body was in the ambulance, then he turned to Melinda, "You should consider having his room cleaned by a professional crew. One that specializes in this kind of thing. Especially now, with all that's going on." He took a card from his pocket and handed it to her. "This company is qualified with the department to do cleanup. We've had good results from them, but you can use anyone you like."

Melinda took the card and thanked him, then I suggested she come home with me to my house. "You could relax for a while and gather yourself."

"Thanks," she said, "but I need to take care of things here." She began crying again but when I tried to hug her, she pushed me away. "I'll be all right," she said. "I just need to be alone." Then she rushed inside and closed the door.

As the ambulance moved up the street away from Bob's house, I started toward home, walking slowly this time and hoping no one came out to ask for details. The death of anyone is a sad occasion, but the death of a neighbor and friend bears its own poignancy. Bob and I were friends. Not like he and Phyllis, but friends all the same. His death weighed heavily on me. I was certain Phyllis would take it much harder, but I wanted to be the one to tell her. I only hoped no one else beat me to her.

Using the extra key from beneath the flowerpot, I let myself into Phyllis' house and walked up the hall toward the staircase, preoccupied with thoughts of what was coming next. The agony. The pain. The grief. As I rounded the end of the banister, I saw Phyllis standing by a window in the corner of the front room. She wore pajamas and a bathrobe with a blanket draped over her shoulders. She turned to me. "Was that Bob in the ambulance?"

"Yes," I replied.

She took a halting step or two in my direction. "How is

he?"

"Phyllis," I said in a somber voice, "Bob is dead."

She stopped abruptly and stared at me a moment, her eyes blank and hollow, then her face twisted into an odd shape like people do when they begin to cry, and she sagged onto a chair. "I knew it," she cried, her hand to her mouth, her chin quivering. "I knew it."

All I could say was, "I am so sorry." I moved next to her, put my arm across her shoulder, and pulled her against me.

"Why is this happening to us?" she sobbed. "Why did this happen to him?"

"I don't know."

She wiped her nose on the blanket. "You go to church. What do they say about things like this?"

"Nothing very satisfying," I said. It was true. People at church had a lot to say about the next life and the relief that comes from knowing what awaits us, but not much to explain how or why things turned out like this, which is what Phyllis was asking about. I knew about evil and choices and all of that, but the illness that took Bob's life didn't have much to do with any of that. Certainly not in a personal sense.

Phyllis looked up at me. "Then what good is all that religion?"

"God is not—"

"Ahh," she scoffed, cutting me off with a dismissive gesture. "I don't want to hear it. Bob never did anything to deserve this." She pushed herself up from the chair and stumbled past me toward the stairs. "And there's no need for you to come around here anymore. I can live or die on my own."

CHAPTER 6

That afternoon, I drove to Jim's house. He hadn't had lunch yet, so I suggested a meal of eggs and toast. Much to my delight, he was able to join me in the kitchen while I prepared it. After the turmoil of the morning, I was overcome with emotion at the sight of him out of bed and moving about the house. So overcome that as he settled onto a chair at the table, I cradled his cheeks in my hands and kissed him on the lips. His breath smelled awful, but I kissed him again, softly. Warmly. I was so glad to see him alive and getting better.

Swept up in the moment, I prepared enough for both of us. Arranged on the plate, that simple meal looked like a feast. I gave Jim the largest portion and watched while he ate. Until then, I'd never known what a joy it was to watch a man consume a meal.

After we finished, we walked into the living room and sat on the sofa beneath a large window that filled the room with sunlight from that late winter, early spring afternoon. Jim held my hand, and we talked a while, then I felt him lean against me. His head rested on my shoulder, and before long his breathing became shallow as he drifted off to sleep. I listened to make sure he was okay, then propped my head against the back of the sofa and joined him for a nap.

Around mid-afternoon, Jim awakened. I helped him upstairs, then waited while he went to the bathroom. When he was finished in there, I escorted him to the bed and tucked him in. A chair was positioned a few feet away, and I took a seat in it. Before long, he was asleep again.

With Jim resting comfortably, I went home to check on Phyllis. Despite what she had said earlier about not coming back, I had no intention of leaving her in that house alone.

When I got upstairs to her bedroom, I found her sprawled on the floor. She was breathing, but barely. Rather than attempting to move her on my own, I called the emergency number and asked for help. Two paramedics arrived within half an hour—longer than their normal response time, but quicker than I expected. Emergency services had been swamped with calls since the virus outbreak.

The paramedics gave her fluids through an IV drip and monitored her where she lay until they determined she was stable, then they called for an ambulance and transported her to the hospital. Phyllis was awake and I could see from the look in her eyes that she was scared. I knew what she was thinking. People go to the hospital when things are bad. Really bad. And with this virus, people were going to the hospital to die. Alone. No visitors. No family members. No friends to hold your hand at the end.

As paramedics carried Phyllis from the house, I saw Allison standing in her front yard. I started toward her, but she held up her hand in protest and said, "Don't come close." I stopped at her driveway, and she said, "What happened to Phyllis? Is she all right?"

"She fell," I said.

"How?"

"I don't know. She was on the floor when I found her."

"Was she conscious?"

"Not when I arrived. The paramedics think she was dehydrated."

"Is she going to make it?"

I didn't know what to say, but I didn't want to speak loud enough for others to hear, so I came closer. Allison inched away. I came even closer. "She was doing well when I saw her this morning," I explained.

"Where will they take her?"

"West Side," I replied.

"Do they have room for her? I heard the hospitals are jammed."

"They're doing the best they can."

"Well, at least she's alive for the ride," Allison said. "Too bad no one was around to check on Bob."

The comment seemed to imply Bob's death was somehow my fault and it flew all over me. "You could have been there for him," I snapped. "You could have checked on him."

"But he was so—"

"Do you think Phyllis wasn't so sick?"

"But she—"

"No," I barked. "You were too afraid to check on either of them. And you told me I shouldn't be around them, either. So don't lament their demise now. And don't blame me for it."

She folded her arms across her chest and cocked her head in an imperious expression. "I don't know what's wrong with you these days. You were—"

"No, no, no," I retorted, wagging my finger at her. "Don't you dare throw that up to me. I'm angry now because you're implying Bob's death was my fault when you could have gone to see about him as easily as anyone."

"I didn't say—"

"You know exactly what you said." My voice was loud and angry. "I've been looking after Jim, and I've been looking after Phyllis and the only reason she was alive enough to get in that ambulance is because I was there. You chose to bury your head in the sand and ignore everyone else but yourself."

"The news says—"

"Damn the news, Allison!" I was shouting by then. "Is that your gospel? Whatever they say on those talk shows. Is that your church now?"

"Gospel? What are you talking about? I thought we were talking about Bob."

"I'm talking about doing what we hear in church—love your neighbor as yourself, care for the sick, feed the hungry— instead of just thinking about it. You chose to think about it and take your real direction from the mindless drivel of a television news show. I did my best to look after our neighbors. I fed the hungry. I visited the sick. So don't blame me if the ones you didn't visit died."

It was a harsh thing to say, and perhaps cruel, but sometimes Allison's penchant for telling everyone else what to do came across as bullying. That's how it seemed that day and I wasn't in the mood for it. She started saying something else, but I didn't wait around to hear the rest. I waved her off with a disgusted gesture and walked away.

The following morning, I received a call from a phone number that wasn't in the contacts list on my phone. Normally, I let those calls roll over to voicemail and, if the caller doesn't leave a message, I block the number. This time, however, I took the call. It was from Phyllis.

"I need you to come get me," she said weakly.

"Where are you?"

"West Side Hospital. But I'm not in the building."

"What do you mean you're not in the building?"

"They had me on a gurney in the hall all night," she said.

"In the hall?" I had heard of similar situations in other hospitals but had no idea it was happening locally.

"Somebody lying across from me died this morning," she said. "Everyone was preoccupied with him so when I got a chance, I unhooked my IV bag from the pole, turned off the infuser pump, and walked outside. A deliveryman let me use his phone. Get over here as quick as you can."

I wasn't sure of the protocol for situations like that. Individuals checked themselves out of medical facilities all the time, but this wasn't like that. Phyllis simply walked out the door. No signature. No paperwork. No reluctant doctor's orders. And she used a deliveryman's phone to call me. That meant she was standing outside. Probably still wearing the pajamas and robe she was wearing the day before. I couldn't leave her like that, so I drove over to the hospital to see about her.

When I arrived, I found Phyllis seated on a bench near the emergency room entrance. As I suspected, she was wearing the clothes she'd had on the day before. I brought the car to a stop across from the bench and came around to help her. She handed me the IV bag while she ducked onto the passenger side of the front seat. "Better hurry," she said as I closed the door. "I don't want them to see me."

I pushed the door closed, then came around to the driver's side. "You're looking better," I said as I got in behind the steering wheel.

"I feel better than I did yesterday." She pointed out the windshield. "Drive. Before they miss me."

I put the car in gear, and we started forward. "Was it bad in there?" I asked.

"It was awful," she said. "Those poor nurses and doctors are working themselves to exhaustion. They have more sick people in there than they have space for. And I don't mean more than they have rooms for. The rooms are full. The ER is full. The units are full. They don't have any more space."

I steered the car toward the street. "Are you sure we should do this?"

"Do what?" she asked.

"Leave like this. Without telling anyone."

"If I tell them I'm going, they'll tell me I can't," Phyllis replied. "It'll just be a fight."

"But you're sick."

"I'm better off at home," she said.

"What about the IV?" The bag and tubing lay in her lap.

"We'll take it out when we get to the house."

"I've never done that," I said.

"I watched them take one out. I'll tell you what to do. There's nothing to it."

When we got to Phyllis' house, she stood at the kitchen sink and told me how to disconnect the hose from the piece in her arm. Then she folded a paper towel and held it near the part that was stuck in her arm. "Okay," she said. "All you do is pinch it between your thumb and index finger and slide it out of the skin. And don't be slow about it. Pull it, but don't snatch it."

"I don't know——"

"It'll be fine," she said, interrupting me. The tone of her voice said she wasn't giving me a choice. "I would do it myself but it's in my right arm and I'm right-handed."

Despite my misgivings, I did as she said and grasped the piece firmly between my fingers, then pulled on it. It resisted at first, then slid freely until it was out. A drop of bright red blood formed where the needle had been inserted into her flesh. Phyllis pressed the folded paper towel over it. "Let's go upstairs so we can put a bandage on it," she said.

I helped her to the staircase, then walked with her up the stairs, all the while wondering why we hadn't started in the bathroom to begin with, but I didn't say anything.

Upstairs, we found bandages and tape in a drawer in the bathroom. I applied it to the place on her arm and pressed it firmly in place. "Did you want to shower?" I asked.

"I'll wait," she said. "I don't want to get the bandage wet right now."

When she was in bed, I went downstairs and prepared the usual tea and toast, then brought it to her on a tray. She ate it without trouble and while she did, we talked.

"Bob was my responsibility," she said. "I can't get over the thought that I let him die."

"You did no such thing," I responded. "He died because

this disease is deadly."

"But if I had been there, looking after him like you're looking after Jim, he might still be here."

"You were too sick to do anything."

"I should have told his daughter."

That much was probably true, but there was no point in dwelling on it. "I don't know the cosmological reasons for his death," I said. "And I don't have theological answers. But I know he didn't die because of you. This disease is deadly. Bob's body couldn't overcome it. And that's all there is to it. You did the best you could."

"There's supposed to be more," she said.

"More of a reason?"

"Yes."

"We want more," I replied. "And we convince ourselves that life is supposed to be a continuous string of happy moments broken rarely and occasionally by brief episodes of sorrow or pain. In reality, life is constant, monotonous sameness interspersed with moments of extreme joy and heartbreaking sorrow. This happens to be a moment of sorrow. But it will pass, and things will get better."

She gave a wan smile. "You mean we will return to boring regularity?"

"Yes," I said. "And we will be thankful for it."

She chuckled. "You're full of it."

"It's as near the truth as you'll find," I said.

"Probably so." She reached for my hand. "I'm sorry I

was rude to you earlier, about Bob."

"I'm sorry you lost him. I know how much he meant to you."

"You're not upset with me?"

She was about to cry, and I was, too. "No," I said. "I'm your friend."

"I'm glad."

"And right now, I'm going downstairs to find something for you to drink." I rose from the chair. "The paramedics said you were dehydrated before. That's why you fell. Without an IV, you'll need to drink more."

"There's a bottle in the cabinet by the refrigerator."

There was a hint of playfulness in her voice, and I responded with a grin. "I don't think you're ready for anything that strong yet."

She turned on her side and pulled the cover over her shoulder. "You spoil all the fun."

I laughed and started downstairs to find a sports drink for her.

On Monday, I received a phone call from Allison's husband, David. "I need you to come over here," he said. "Allison isn't doing too well."

"She told me not to," I replied. He sounded worried but I thought I should tell him she didn't want me around.

"I know," he said. "But I think you should come over anyway. She's not doing well."

Reluctantly, I dressed and went across the street to their house. David met me at the front door and led me to the den. It was a wonderful room. A wall of windows looked onto the pool and yard with the giant oak tree in the corner where I had stood with Jim at the party. Most of the furniture was arranged to take advantage of the view. Allison was seated in a chair, staring blankly toward the yard.

"Allison," I said. "What's the matter?"

When she didn't respond, David said, "She's been like this since yesterday. Just sitting in that chair, staring out the window."

I moved a chair close to her and sat down. She still didn't

respond so I reached over and rested my hand on hers. We sat there in silence for what seemed like a long time, then I noticed tears on her cheeks.

"What's the matter?" I asked again. "Tell me."

She slowly turned to look at me. "It's my fault," she said.

"What's your fault?"

"Phyllis," she sobbed. "Jim. Bob. It's all my fault."

"What are you talking about?"

Her eyes narrowed in a pained expression. "Phyllis and Jim got sick because of that party. And Bob died because of it."

"You don't know that," I said.

"That's what everyone is saying."

"Everyone?" I asked. "Who's saying that?"

"Melinda," she replied.

"Bob's daughter?"

"She called me yesterday. Yelling and crying and screaming. She said if I hadn't been such a know-it-all and a busybody, Bob would still be alive."

"Who else said that?"

"Janice."

"Janice is a gossip," I replied. It was true. She never avoided passing on the latest rumor, whether it was true or not. I confronted her about it once and she told me she didn't care if what she said was true or not. That she wasn't vouching for it, just passing along what someone had said. I made sure not to tell her anything of consequence after that.

"Who else?" I asked.

"Linda."

"Linda couldn't find her way to the store if her husband drove her."

David laughed. Allison smiled, but the smile quickly faded. "They say I gave everyone the virus by having that party."

"They're idiots," I said. "Do you have the virus?"

"No."

"Does David have the virus?"

"No," she said. "But Phyllis and Bob and Jim were all at the party. At our house."

"They are all adults, too," I noted. "If they thought it was too risky, they could have stayed home. Gladys stayed home. She told me it was too risky to get together. That's why she didn't come." Gladys was the oldest person in the neighborhood.

Allison squeezed my hand. "You've been around all of them."

"Yes."

"And you don't have it."

"Not yet."

"What does that mean?"

"For one thing, it takes up to two weeks to develop," I said. "But listen, Bob was the first to have symptoms and Phyllis told me he was not feeling well that night."

"The night of the party?"

"Yes."

Allison frowned. "So, everyone's right. That party made them all sick."

"It might have been the place where Jim and Phyllis were exposed, but it didn't have anything to do with making Bob sick. He was already sick when he arrived. And if that's how Jim got sick, why didn't I get sick then, too? I was standing right there with them."

"But you weren't next to Bob."

"We can quibble about this all day," I said. "But the fact remains. Everyone at that party was an adult. They could have stayed home if they had wanted to."

"Do you think we should have canceled it?"

Hindsight is useless for discussions like that. If she had planned the party for a date three weeks later, we all would have objected. But that's not what happened. The party happened in the gray period, before lockdowns and slowdowns, at a time when politicians were blaming each other, and every person with an opportunity appeared on television with some quack remedy. There was no point in discussing any of that with her. Instead, I turned to David. "She needs a soft drink," I said. "Something with sugar in it."

"I'm not sure we have any," he replied. "We usually have diet drinks."

"Sugar," I insisted. "She needs sugar."

Allison caught his eye. "There's a bottle of cola in the pantry."

David left the room and when he was out of earshot, I leaned over to Allison. "What's done, is done. You're not to blame for any of this. Bob's daughter is upset because she didn't check on him for almost a week. She didn't want to be there, so she let Phyllis take care of him, but then Phyllis got sick and couldn't get out of bed to look after him. By the time Melinda found out about it, Bob had been by himself for several days."

Allison frowned. "So, Melinda's to blame?"

"I'm not blaming anyone for anything. I'm just saying, that's what Melinda's upset about. Bob was sick and she didn't want to be around him. Phyllis loved him and was going to look after him anyway. It was easier for Melinda to let her do it than to come over there every day and take care of him. But Phyllis got sick—probably from being around him—and she was really sick. Too sick to go up there. And too sick to think about calling Melinda. But Melinda would have known all that if she had been coming to see her father more often than once a week."

"Did Phyllis pick up the virus at the party?"

I gave her a knowing look. "Phyllis got that virus from Bob. They had been together constantly up to that point."

She raised an eyebrow. "Together?"

"In a Biblical sense."

Allison chuckled. "They're too old for that."

"Are you too old for it?"

"No," she said. "But I'm married."

"Phyllis doesn't have that boundary in her life."

"We need to get her to church."

"She needs an encounter with the Holy Spirit, but she's a few steps away from that, still."

"I saw you bring her back," Allison said. "They let her out of the hospital already?"

"She let herself out," I replied.

"She checked herself out?"

I shook my head. "She walked out."

"No." Allison appeared startled. "She didn't."

"Yes, she did. She called me to come get her. I found her on a bench behind the hospital with her IV bag in her hand."

"Ha!" Allison laughed. "You've been good to her." She patted my hand. "You've kept Jim and Phyllis alive."

"I've been trying."

David arrived with two glasses of cola. I watched while Allison took a sip. "Have some more," I said, pointing to her glass. She took a longer sip.

"I talked to Jim this morning." Allison paused to take another drink. "He sounded good. Said he made his own breakfast."

My heart skipped a beat. In all the flurry about Phyllis and getting her from the hospital and removing the IV, I had completely forgotten about Jim.

Late that afternoon I rode to Jim's house. He met me at the door, dressed in slacks and a t-shirt. "You're up and moving," I said as I stepped inside.

"Thought I should try," he said. "Not sure for how long, though."

"You've been in bed several days," I noted. "Don't try to do too much."

We kissed in the hallway, then he took my hand and led me to the sofa in the front room where we sat together. "What have you been doing today?" he asked.

"I picked up Phyllis from the hospital and then spent the last hour or two talking to Allison."

He looked concerned. "Phyllis was in the hospital?"

"I found her on the floor yesterday," I replied. "She was in bad shape. I called the paramedics. They had an ambulance take her."

"The hospital only kept her for one day?"

"She left."

His eyes opened wider. "On her own?"

"Called me to come get her."

"How is she now?"

"She was fine when I saw her this morning."

"You didn't check on her this afternoon?"

"I had to see about Allison. Then I came to see about you."

"What's wrong with Allison?"

"She's feeling guilty about the party," I explained.

"What about it makes her feel guilty?"

"You and Phyllis and Bob got sick."

"And she thinks it had something to do with the party?"

"Some of the neighbors are telling her that. I think it all started with Bob's daughter."

He looked perturbed. "Bob's daughter is accusing Allison of something?"

"Venting," I said. "Mostly. I think she feels guilty. She thought Phyllis was taking care of him, but Phyllis got sick, and Bob was in the house for several days by himself."

"But Allison didn't make anyone sick."

"No. And Bob had a telephone. He could have called for help."

"I imagine Allison was devastated by the suggestion she did something wrong."

"Completely."

"But why do they think any of this was her fault?"

"As best I can figure it out, Bob was already sick when he came to the party. Phyllis got it from him, either at the party or before. You probably picked it up from him at the party, too. I'm not sure if anyone else did."

"But Bob didn't get it there."

"According to the working theory, he's the one who brought it to the party."

"Ha!" Jim laughed. "It's not funny that he died but the way you said it. Like he brought a bottle of wine. Only in this case, a virus."

I smiled. "They say this is how it spreads. Through personal contact."

He squeezed me closer. "Then you should be sickest of all."

I rested my head on his shoulder. "I don't care if I get sick or not. I just want to be with you."

CHAPTER 8

On Tuesday of the following week, I awakened feeling lethargic and disinterested. By noon I was achy and tired like I often experienced with the flu. I had to force myself to check on Phyllis and Jim and spent most of the day propped in the chair in my bedroom. By evening, my throat was sore, and I had an elevated temperature. Not too high. Just enough to make me feel unwell. At first, I refused to believe it was caused by the virus and tried to soothe my throat with lozenges and hot tea.

When I awakened on Friday, I forced myself to get out of bed and brew a pot of coffee. While sipping it, I noticed I had lost my sense of taste which was one of the symptoms caused by the virus. That's when I went to be tested. On Tuesday of the following week, they telephoned with the results. I had COVID-19. By then, the symptoms were bad enough that I knew it already before they gave me the official results.

Most of the people I knew who had contracted the virus reacted to it in fear. A few tried some of the home remedies making the rounds of various fringe websites. Odd as it may sound, I was relieved to learn I had it. As if having COVID indicated I was normal—part of the new normal, as people were describing our virus-aware life. Phyllis and Bob and Jim had it and by the time I tested positive for it, most of us knew others outside our immediate group of friends who had it. My internal psyche seemed to need it, too. To be like the others. To fit in and be one of the group. It was a high schoolish reaction, I know, but that's how I felt.

At first, I had the energy to push on through and do a few things at home, but because of Jim's improving condition, I avoided visiting him out of concern that he might catch the virus again. I didn't know if it was possible—no one seemed to know much about that aspect of the virus—but I didn't want to find out by mistake and ruin things for him. He understood my concern.

News of my condition spread quickly to those who lived on our block. Most of them shook their heads in pity as if to say, "I told you so." None offered to help in any way. If I could have talked to them, I would have berated them for living in fear and complacency, and for their condescending attitude toward those of us who tried to help, but that probably would have been counterproductive. Fear is so debilitating and complacency so entrenching, my yelling would have only reinforced their existing attitudes. And it would have been the opposite of forgiveness, which is the response I'd been learning.

As my symptoms grew worse, I struggled against feeling

abandoned and, had it not been for Allison, I might have plunged beneath the waves of despair, but I did not, and it was largely due to her courage and renewed sense of selflessness. She called and checked on me morning and night. And when I became sicker and didn't feel like preparing anything to eat, she placed a Styrofoam cooler by my front door and kept it stocked with casseroles she'd taken from her freezer.

There came a day, however, when even Allison's attention proved no match for the virus, and I was forced to bed. My temperature soared, eventually becoming so high I stopped checking it. Day blended with night, sleep with wakefulness, then the days and nights disappeared altogether, and I lapsed into a cycle marked only by varying degrees of consciousness.

Dream tumbled atop dream in a fitful series of nonsensical images, but eventually, the fever lifted, and I awakened to find Allison seated in a chair by my bed. She wore two masks over her nose and mouth, double rubber gloves on each hand, and a face shield for added safety, but she was right there at my side. "You're awake," she said with a smile.

"I'm not sure," I replied. "I think it might still be a dream." Her appearance made me wonder.

"You were rather delirious at one point," she noted. "I thought we might have to call the paramedics."

"I'm glad you didn't."

"David said we should wait. He didn't think you would like the hospital any more than Phyllis."

David was right. I wouldn't have. "How is Phyllis?" I asked.

"She's out of bed and taking care of herself," Allison said. "But she's still not well enough to get out of the house."

"And Jim?"

"He's doing good. Not completely recovered but much better. I sent him to the grocery store for Phyllis yesterday."

That didn't seem like a good idea, but I avoided complaining. She was trying to do the right thing. "You didn't let him in her house, did you?" I don't know why that bothered me. If he went to the grocery store, he would have been exposed to far more than anything living inside Phyllis' house.

"No," she said. "I had him put it on the porch."

I glanced around the room. "How long have I been in here like this?"

"In bed?"

"Yes."

"About a week," she said. "I think."

"A week. That's a long time. I have no memory of even going to the bathroom." In that much time, surely at least one bodily function would have taken me in there.

Allison grinned. "We had to work at it."

"You got me up?"

"Yes," she replied.

Imagining what that must have been like was disconcerting—the sights, the sounds … the wiping. I changed the subject. "How did you get in the house?"

"I know where you keep an extra key," she said.

There were two, though I wasn't sure she knew that. One was under the front steps and the other was behind the cover for the dryer vent near the back door. "I thought you said we shouldn't do this," I commented. "Going inside each other's houses while we were sick." I don't know why I said it. I was glad she was there.

"You taught me that we should act differently from that," she responded.

A lump caught in my throat at the suggestion I had taught her something. It took me by surprise, and I had to swallow hard to choke down the emotion. "If we go down," I said, "we go down loving our neighbors as ourselves." That was what I had said to her when the pandemic first appeared.

"Exactly." Allison took a bowl from the nightstand. "I made you some soup. It's mostly broth. I think you should try it."

She spooned some into my mouth and I was relieved that I could taste it. "This is very good," I said. Normally, I would have noticed the lack of salt in her food but that day I didn't, which told me I still wasn't well—my sense of taste hadn't returned yet.

"You sound surprised," she said.

"No," I responded. "Just glad." With no sense of taste, I was going on good manners. I'd had her soup before, and it wasn't nearly as good as her casserole, but she was kind enough to bring it to me. I thought it only right to offer a compliment. I took another spoonful, then rested my head on the pillow. "You said I was delirious?"

"From the fever," she answered. "Your temperature was high."

"Did I say anything unnecessary or … stupid?" The thought that I might have said something ridiculous was unsettling.

"No." She laughed. "Nothing like that."

"What did I say?"

"Just something about 'she has beautiful legs.'"

I remembered a dream about that. "Stephanie," I said. "The assistant."

"I had a dream about attending their wedding. Everyone was there. Even you and—" Allison looked sad. I was worried. "What's the matter?"

"There isn't going to be a wedding," she said softly.

It was an odd comment and I wondered how she would be privy to that kind of information. "No wedding? Why not?"

"Walt had COVID." Allison's voice was low and her eyes sad.

News that Walt had contracted the virus hit me hard. In all my scurrying around caring for Phyllis and Jim, then with Bob dying and Allison feeling guilty, I hadn't thought of Walt at all. The notion never crossed my mind that he or Stephanie might be sick.

"Had?" I asked. "What are you saying?" They were rhetorical questions. I knew what she was saying but I wanted her to tell me the details.

"He didn't make it," she replied.

My eyes opened wide. "He died?"

Walt was an athletic man. Always active and quite robust. If anyone could have withstood this illness, I would have expected it to be him.

"Yes," Allison said. "He passed away earlier this week."

"Walt has died?" I wanted to be sure.

"Yes."

Despite the way I'd felt toward Walt, I never wanted him to die and now that he had, the sense of loss was overwhelming. It was an odd moment. He had betrayed me in the worst way and hurt me deeper than anyone could imagine, but I hadn't wished him dead. Earlier, I would have thought it was too easy an escape for him. Hardly a year ago I wanted him to live a long life and pay dearly every day for the misery he'd brought me.

More recently, though, having worked toward forgiving Walt, and Stephanie, I had been curious about how their situation might work out. The challenges they would face and the creative solutions they would find. He was at least twice her age, which is a lot of difference at any stage in life but at ours, it could prove insurmountable.

And what of Stephanie? She was pregnant with Walt's baby and alive in ways I had never known, thinking of all the possibilities that lay before her, the baby, them. And with no warning whatsoever, he was taken away, leaving her with the task of raising their child alone. "That's awful," I said, and I genuinely meant it. "How is Stephanie?"

"I think she's okay," Allison replied. "I haven't talked to her other than the one time."

"One time?"

"There was a message on your phone asking you to call her," Allison explained. "I called her back and that's when she told me about Walt."

"I suppose she's living in his house."

"Not right now," Allison said. "At least, she wasn't when we talked."

"Then where is she?"

"After Walt tested positive for the virus, she moved into a house on Chelsea Street in Bellaire."

"We own two down there," I said.

Bellaire was a separate municipality, not far from Rice University. Several houses there had been damaged in a hurricane. We bought them at a discount, made the necessary repairs and upgrades, then rented them out. The long-term plan had been to tear them down and construct something else in their place, but Walt liked the steady income from the rent, so we delayed doing anything with them.

"I don't know the specific address," Allison said. "The doctor told her it would not be good for the baby if she got COVID while she was pregnant. So, she moved out when

Walt tested positive."

Then the thought of all that needed to be done at the office came crashing down on top of me. Bills. Bids. Payroll. The pandemic had disrupted parts of our business but not all of it. We had projects in various stages of development with contracts in place that could not be avoided. "I need to get out of this bed," I said.

Allison looked concerned. "Why?"

"We need to find Walt's will. Who knows what he did with his half of the business."

"You think she owns his part?"

"He couldn't have made her my partner," I replied. "Not officially. I think that could only happen with my consent. But he could have left her the financial interest of his half."

Allison shook her head. "You need to stay right there in bed. I'm sure someone at the office can look after things."

"But that's the question," I said. "Are they? Stephanie might have been good at looking after Walt, at a certain level, but that girl knows very little about the real estate investment business."

I reached for the cover to roll it out of the way, but Allison stopped me. "Why don't you call someone? There must be someone who can fill you in on the details. A lawyer, maybe? An accountant?"

Exposing my leg to the air sent a chill up my spine. Maybe she was right. Maybe I should begin with a phone call.

Allison took my phone from the nightstand and handed

it to me. I phoned the office bookkeeper and, after a brief discussion about Walt, asked for the latest financial reports. When I finished with him, I contacted the accountant's office and requested a copy of their monthly reports. With that in motion, I propped up in bed and used my laptop to access records for the bank accounts from our bank's website.

By the time I had read through the bank records, the previous month's reports had arrived from the bookkeeper and the accountant. I spent the evening reading them and comparing the information. All appeared in order, but I was uncomfortable with the lack of hands-on control. Who made the decisions? Were decisions even being made? My mind raced. I needed to be at the office, but I still was too weak to get out of bed.

The following day, I forced myself out of bed and sat in the chair in the corner of the room. I re-read the financial reports, then logged onto the company server and worked through the project files that had been loaded onto it. Not everything was there but enough to tell me where we were with our pending projects—a development on the west side that we were marketing and selling, an apartment complex under construction near midtown, a planned community on the south side we started as a sandbox for ideas, and, to the northwest, the one Walt and I had dreamed about.

A few phone calls to our managers and supervisors seemed to assure them, and me, that I was in control. It wasn't the role I had foreseen for myself. Since Allison's party, I had been thinking of selling my interest in the business to Walt and letting him have the whole thing. That wasn't possible now. Someone had to run the business. That job seemed to have chosen me.

At noon, I went downstairs to the kitchen to brew myself a cup of tea. Negotiating the stairs was an arduous task, more so than I imagined, and I had to rest at the kitchen table before proceeding, but once the tea was ready and I had a few sips, I felt better. I found a package of crackers on the counter beside me. They weren't the brand I normally bought. I assumed they came from Allison. I opened the package and nibbled on one between sips of tea. Allison had left soup in the refrigerator, so I had a bowl of that, too. This time, I noticed she'd omitted the salt, which I took as a sign that I was getting better.

After an hour in the kitchen, I was ready to return to bed. I made my way from the kitchen to the staircase and stared up at the second floor. It seemed the stairs were a steep mountain towering into the sky. For a moment I considered lying on the sofa in the front room, but there was only a throw for cover, and I was certain that would not be enough. Reluctantly, I grasped the handrail and took the first step.

Climbing to the top proved more of a challenge than coming down had been, but not as difficult as it had first appeared. Taking one step at a time, I was able to reach the second floor without incident, though I was winded from the climb and my legs felt heavy. When I made it to the bed, I fell over on it, face first still with my housecoat wrapped around me, and went to sleep.

CHAPTER 9

A few days later, I contacted our business attorney, Paul Menefee, and arranged to see him that afternoon. He'd been our attorney for business issues since the beginning and we continued to use him during and after the divorce. Neither of us trusted anyone else to help with the legal arrangements of our business and there was no one else I wanted to guide me through the process of managing it now that Walt was gone. Paul's office was in a downtown high-rise on Louisiana Street. Negotiating traffic on my own seemed overwhelming, so I asked Allison to drive me. She readily agreed.

Paul was an intelligent man, and a pleasant person to talk to. I always enjoyed the time we spent with him. That day, he was especially pleasant and spent the first twenty minutes of our meeting reminiscing about Walt and things that happened in our younger days. We'd all known each other since before Walt and I married. Finally, though, he turned to the matter at hand. "You wanted to discuss your business arrangements," he said.

"Yes," I replied. "As you know, we have several ongoing

projects. And despite the pandemic and all that has happened, none of it has come to a complete stop. Someone has to look after it and with Walt being sick toward the end, I'm not sure how well things have been managed or what it will be like going forward. I wanted to touch on some of it with you and see what you could tell me about where we are with it."

He smiled. "I don't think anything is out of hand. And I think you'll find the business a little easier to manage than you imagined. At least in one respect."

That seemed like a strange comment. "Oh? How so?"

"After your divorce, Walt asked me about changing his will. I told him that was a good idea, given that the legal privileges of his marital status had changed, but I didn't feel comfortable discussing the matter with him. When it comes to estate planning, former husbands and former wives don't share many common interests. If I had attempted to advise him about what was best for him, I might have needed to tell him something that wasn't in your best interest. That would create a conflict of interest for me and perhaps disqualify me from working with either of you on any matter."

"Did he understand that?" When Walt made up his mind about something, he could be difficult to deal with until he got his way. It wasn't hard to imagine him trying to coerce Paul into helping him, regardless of Paul's misgivings.

"He pushed back some," Paul replied. "But I told him just what I've said to you, that I wasn't choosing sides between the two of you and if he forced me to, I would refuse to represent either of you on anything. He assured me that wouldn't be a problem and I agreed to meet with him, to hear what he had to say, under the provision that I wasn't prohibited from discussing his plans with you, regardless of whether I wrote his will or did anything else regarding his personal affairs. I even made him sign a release to that effect."

That was typical of Paul. Always playing it straight. "So, he agreed to that?" I asked.

"Yes," Paul replied. "In fact, he was eager to sign the release and tell me what he wanted to do."

"What did he want to do?"

Paul opened a file, and I could see the release was the document on top. He moved it aside to reveal Walt's will beneath it. "He placed his personal investments—cash, stocks, that sort of thing—the house he occupied, and the contents, in a trust for the support of Stephanie and their child, but he left his portion of the business to you." He handed me a copy of the will.

I was stunned. The entire business. To me. I could hardly think and glanced at the document as I tried to recover. After a moment, I looked at Paul. "He gave me his half of the business?" It was all I could think to say.

Paul nodded. "He said you worked as hard for it as he did. And whatever you did with it, you would do the right thing."

Tears filled my eyes. My lip quivered and I put my hand

to my mouth to cover it. "I don't know how to respond to that," I said. Generosity wasn't Walt's primary character trait. He wasn't mean. He just wasn't the type to think of giving as a first response.

Paul reached across the desk and took my hand. "I was surprised, too," he said.

"Any hint of why he did it?"

He let go of my hand and leaned away from the desk. "I don't think he trusted anyone else to take care of the business the way he would have. I think continuing to operate it with you after the divorce convinced him you would do the right thing, even if you didn't like it."

I took a deep breath. Paul offered a tissue. I took it and wiped my eyes. "He couldn't have made anyone else my partner, could he?"

"No. He couldn't. The business was a general partnership. He could have left his financial participation to someone else. That person could have received his right to the income, and to the balance in his equity account at liquidation, but they wouldn't have been your partner in managing the business. Walt couldn't force someone on you in that manner." He closed the file that lay on his desk. "But you don't have to worry about that now. The business is yours entirely."

"Has the probate process been started?"

"We've filed the petition and sent the required notices. You should receive yours in the mail shortly. He named Victor as executor."

Vic was Walt's brother. We got along well. I didn't foresee any trouble, but still, you never know. "Are you the attorney for the estate?" I asked.

"Yes," he replied.

That made me feel better. "Have you talked to Stephanie?"

"Vic has. I don't think she'll be a problem."

"What about the child?"

"What about it?"

I bristled at the impersonal reference. The child was a living person. He or she. Or a personal nonbinary reference. Or anything other than it. I let the issue pass and said, "Will that be a problem? Doesn't she or he have an interest in Walt's estate?"

"That's why we created the trust."

"And everyone's satisfied with that?"

"I believe so."

The issue of Walt's child and his or her relationship with Walt's estate bothered me. I knew from past dealings with the legal system that a child's financial interest can't be fully resolved until the child reaches adulthood and I wondered how that applied to this situation.

After worrying about that for a few days, I drove myself to the house on Chelsea Street where Stephanie lived. I wasn't sure if she would be home, or whether she would answer the doorbell, but she did and let me inside. We sat in the front room. I sat on the sofa. She sat in an armchair.

"I was sorry to hear about Walt," I began. "I was sick when he died and didn't hear about it until several days later."

"Thank you," she replied. "I called you and left a message. Your neighbor called me back. She told me you were ill."

"I suppose we should be honest about how strange this is," I said. "You as his fiancé. Me as his former wife." We had no hope of working things out between us if we didn't acknowledge our situation and address it in a straightforward manner.

She seemed uncomfortable and shifted positions in the chair. "About that," she began. "I feel I should tell you how sorry I am for the way things happened between me and Walt. I'm not sorry about how I felt toward him, or how he felt toward me, but I am sorry that things between us … happened the way they happened."

"You mean, me walking in on the two of you?"

"Yes." She blushed. "And just that whole aspect of it."

I assumed she meant the physical nature of their relationship, the sneaking around to downtown hotels, him lying to me about working late or attending a conference, but I thought dwelling on those things would only stir up trouble. We were never going to unravel it all and make it go away.

"Thank you for that," I said. "I appreciate it." She was try-ing. I needed to acknowledge her effort.

"I know it was painful for you," she continued. "I can't even imagine how deeply it must have hurt."

I pressed my lips together and nodded. She seemed inter-ested in dwelling on the topic. I was not. "And now you have a child on the way."

"Yes." She patted her belly. "Coming soon."

"Do you know the gender?"

"No. They asked if I wanted to know, but I told them I would rather wait. I have been referring to her as her, but I don't know, one way or the other." She used a personal pro-noun for the baby. I liked that.

There was an awkward silence, then I said, "I under-stand Walt was cremated."

She nodded. "I wanted them to wait until you were well, but they said with the pandemic and all that they didn't want to hold his body."

"What did you do with his ashes?"

"I have them." She pointed over her shoulder. "They're in an urn in the dining room."

It struck me as morbidly humorous—human remains in a room where meals were consumed—but I didn't laugh. "Makes for an interesting dinner atmosphere," I said dryly.

"I don't use that room for eating," she noted. "The table is covered with stuff anyway."

An image flashed through my mind of how my own dining table used to look. "What do you plan to do with them?"

"The things on the table?"

"The ashes," I said.

"I thought you might have some ideas for that," she replied. "I suppose we could put them in the garden at the other house."

"His house?" I asked. "The one where you and he were living before?"

"Yes. The one on Vassar Street where Walt moved during the divorce."

"I don't know. Everything seems so transient now," I said. "It's difficult to know what might happen to that house. We never had a permanent place. Everything we ever owned was subject to sale or demolition to make room for something else."

"You mean if it was sold, or something?"

"Yes."

"Would it matter if someone else lived there?"

"I suppose not," I replied. "But it might if they tore down the house and built a new one that covered the place where we put his ashes."

She seemed to understand. "I guess we could put them in a mausoleum."

Ah. Yes. I had forgotten that. "Our church has a columbarium," I offered.

She seemed puzzled. "What's that?"

"A mausoleum for ashes."

"You pour them out there?"

I shook my head. "It's like a wall with compartments. You put the urn inside one of them and it has a piece that covers the opening with a plaque on the outside that has the person's information."

"Oh." Her countenance brightened. "That might be good. Not much chance it will get torn down and hauled away."

"And if they do, I'm sure they would move everything to an appropriate location."

"Perhaps we could go there together to see it before we decide."

"I would appreciate that," I replied. Appreciate seemed the right response. It didn't seem correct to say that I would enjoy it, though I thought I would. There was another awkward silence, then I said, "They told you about the business."

She nodded. "That he left it to you?"

"Yes."

"Paul Menefee told me." There was a hint of disappointment in her voice but not anger.

"Do you plan to continue to work?"

"I'm not sure what I could do," she said. "But I suppose I will. I'll need health insurance for me and the baby and having a job is the best way to get that."

It was awkward for me to tell her I wanted her to stay and continue to work for me, but that's what I wanted. Sitting with her and talking, I was filled with empathy for her, and for the child she was carrying. According to the way things work in life, I was supposed to be angry with her and cut her off in every direction. That was the trope. That was the stereotypical response. But I didn't feel that way and I was reminded of a time when Jesus met a woman who'd been caught in adultery. He was kind to her, not judgmental or harsh. I felt kindness toward Stephanie. "You could keep doing what you've been doing," I said.

A smile teased the corners of her mouth. "You mean, work for you?"

"Yes. I'm sure most of what's on your dining room table is documents from the office."

"Yes," she responded. "I've been working from home a lot. Everyone has. You saw that when you were down there that day. I've been working from here since Walt got sick." She looked over at me. "Wouldn't that be difficult? Both of us in the same office. Together. What would people think?"

"I don't care what the others think," I replied. "And as for you and me, we could work things out between us, if we wanted to."

Stephanie smiled, "I would like that very much. I enjoy working in the business." She glanced around the room. "What about this house? Will you want us to move out?"

"Do you like it here?"

"Yes," she said. "I do."

"Then we'll add that to your salary package."

Stephanie's eyes focused on mine. "You're being very

generous to me."

"There's a lot up in the air right now. Having you in place would be helpful." I could have told her more—about learning to forgive and how the practice of forgiveness was empowering my life—but she wasn't ready to hear that, and I wasn't ready to say it, either.

"Do you intend to run the business full-time?" she asked.

"I don't think I have a choice," I replied.

"I suppose not."

We sat in silence for a moment, then I said, "You'll need some sort of daycare for the baby, eventually. Or at least some help."

"Yes," she said. "For the days I come to the office."

"We can work that out when the time comes. But tell me something. You said you liked the work. Do you like the real estate business?"

"Yes. I do," she replied. "And I think I was beginning to understand what you and Walt were doing."

"Then, as long as that's the case, we'll find a way to make this work."

I left Stephanie's feeling full and clean and wonderful for the first time in five years. Probably longer than that. It seemed as if a great weight had been lifted from me. A cloud over my head had dissipated. A dark abyss had been removed from my sight. Forgiveness was not about repressing one's anger and resentment but about turning an enemy into a friend. The only way that can occur is through forgiveness, relationship, and loving others as we love ourselves.

Less than six months had passed since Allison's party. Yet it seemed I had been on a long journey to a foreign land. A journey that transformed me along the way so that I arrived in that land no longer a foreigner, but a native. The pandemic had posed grave risks, but it had proved to be a transformational experience, too.

CHAPTER 10

After talking to Stephanie, I drove straight to Jim's house. I wanted to tell him about all that had happened and the way I'd felt after talking to Stephanie. He met me at the door, and we sat together on the sofa in the front room. I told him about my visit with Paul and about my plan to employ Stephanie to help me. "I think she could do quite well in the real estate business, eventually." He listened attentively but I could see that something was bothering him. "What's the matter?" I asked.

"I've been talking with my son," he said. "Almost every day since I became sick. He wants to move to New Orleans."

"Oh." Sadness filled my heart. From the way he spoke, I was convinced Jim wanted to do it. "Have the two of you made plans for the move?"

"Yes," he said. "Sort of."

The sadness I'd felt evaporated. He had obviously been considering the move for quite a while, and yet, even with all that we had experienced together in the past few months, this was the first he had said anything to me about it. "Sort of?" I asked.

"I haven't purchased a home," he replied.

"But you want to."

"Yes." He squeezed my hand. "And I want you to come with me."

I had been to New Orleans many times and I never cared for it, not as a place to live. The food was good, the culture interesting, and the history engaging, but the prospect of living there … Most areas of the city looked damp to me, perhaps only a few feet above sea level at most. And the air always seemed musty and heavy.

"I can't," I whispered. "I have a business to run."

"You could sell it." He spoke in that self-assured, almost flippant, tone that men use when they talk to a woman whom they think is incapable of serious thought. As if to say, You could sell it, stupid. I hated it when men spoke to me like that.

"We have projects that aren't complete," I said. My back was up, but I didn't want to raise my voice.

"Those were Walt's projects," he replied.

It was a reference to the incident in my dining room and the papers on the table. How dare he throw that up to me.

"They're my projects, too," I said. "Contracts are involved. Obligations have been made. People's livelihoods depend on the work."

"Someone else could buy it and take over all that."

Not only did he want me to move away from everything

and everyone I'd known my entire adult life, but he also wanted me to sell my business. What about Stephanie? And the baby? A sense of moral urgency took the place of everything else I'd felt.

"And what about the child?" I asked.

"It's Walt's baby," he groused. "Not yours." He used that condescending tone again. The one that meant, It's Walt's baby, stupid. How could I explain the situation with Stephanie to someone like that? How could I make him see that this wasn't about Walt, but about me and living the life Jesus talked about?

"I've spent most of the last year learning to forgive," I said. "Learning what it means to love my neighbor as myself. Placing myself in harm's way for the sake of others, including you. I'm not turning my back on that now."

"You're being naïve," he responded. "You would be doing the girl a service if you let her survive on her own. Let her bear the consequences and responsibility for her own actions. It's the only way she'll learn from it."

He was trying to bully me. "I didn't do that with you," I said. "I didn't leave you to bear the results of your own decisions."

"What do you mean?" He let go of my hand and leaned away. "You think I gave myself the virus?"

"Somewhere in the chain of events, you made a choice that exposed you to it. Attending the party. Being near Bob. Being around someone else. The grocery store. The coffee shop. Whatever. Going to those places was the result of decisions you made. Should I have let you lie upstairs in misery so you could learn from it?"

"A baby is not a virus." His voice was sullen and angry. "And it didn't come into existence through casual contact."

Anger that had been simmering since our conversation boiled over. "I know very well how that baby came into existence. And I know something else. That baby isn't a consequence. She's a living, breathing person. And whether you like it or not, I have the power to bless her, and I'm going to do just that. She didn't ask to be here. She had nothing to do with how she got here. But if I choose, I can have everything to do with helping her find her way. And that's a choice I'm going to take."

He smirked at me. "You haven't given up on it, have you."

"On what?"

"On having Walt's baby."

That was it for me. There was nothing more for us to talk about. I wanted to slap him, yell at him, scream at him. Instead, I stood. "I was mistaken about you," I said.

"How so?"

"I thought you were a better man than this." I walked to the door. "I hope you enjoy your life in New Orleans, but don't ever call me again."

❖　❖　❖

When I arrived home, I put the car in the garage and started toward the back door. As I turned to step onto the back porch, a light from Phyllis' kitchen window caught my eye. I needed to talk to someone, to tell them what had happened. So, I crossed the driveway and knocked on her back door. She let me inside and we sat at the kitchen table.

"You don't look so good," she said.

"It's been a long afternoon."

"Trouble?"

"Yes."

She glanced at the clock. "Is it too late for you to drink coffee?"

"I would love some," I replied.

While the coffee brewed, she brought a cake from the pantry. "Cathy from up the street sent this to me." She set it on the table. "I'm not sure if it's any good."

"How old is it?"

"She brought it yesterday."

"Then I guess it depends on how long she had it before she sent it to you."

Phyllis laughed. "I'm sure she baked it."

"Then we should be thankful and enjoy it."

Phyllis set plates on the table, and I cut a slice for us. When the coffee was ready, she filled my cup and then took a seat across from me. "Okay," she said. "Tell me what happened."

Without too much detail, I told her about my visit with

Stephanie and about my interest in keeping her involved in the business. She was glad I did that. Then I told her about my conversation with Jim. She was appalled but before we'd discussed it very much, there was a knock at the front door. When Phyllis answered it, I heard Allison's voice. They came to the kitchen and Phyllis poured her a cup of coffee.

Allison took a seat at the table and glanced at me. "I saw you come over here and wanted to join you."

"I'm glad you did," I replied.

"I talked to Jim."

They must have been closer than I realized. "What did he have to say?" I knew what he had to say, but I wanted her to tell it.

"He told me about your conversation."

"Is he still angry?"

"He thinks you need counseling."

That made me angry all over again. "He said that?"

"Yes."

"What did you say to that?"

"I told him he needed to grow up and stop being a bully."

"Ha!" I laughed out loud. "You said that?"

"Yes, I did."

Phyllis shook her head. "I had no idea he was like that."

I took a sip of coffee. "I don't think anyone did."

"I hate it when men talk down to me," Allison said. "Some of them do it in the subtlest of ways. You hardly notice it when they're talking, they make it sound so wise and all-knowing. And then you get home and realize, he just called me stupid!"

"Exactly," I said.

"David tried that with me when we were first married," Allison responded.

Phyllis grinned. "What did you do?"

"I pinned him against the wall and told him if he ever talked to me that way again, he'd be waking up in a ditch trying to remember his name."

"You did not," I laughed.

"Yes, I did."

"What did he say to that?"

Allison grinned. "He kissed me and carried me to the bedroom."

"I bet he said the same thing the next day," Phyllis said.

"Nope." Allison shook her head. "He never talked to me like that again."

We talked our way through the pot of coffee and considered making more, but Allison had to go home. When she was gone, Phyllis and I prepared supper and as we ate together, I thought about how the day had gone with Paul and Stephanie. And how it had ended with Walt. And then to be with Phyllis and Allison.

The next morning, I phoned Stephanie and arranged to

meet her at the church that afternoon to view the columbarium. Phyllis and Allison went with me. Our priest was there, too—I phoned him earlier and asked him to join us—and he gave us a tour.

There wasn't much to see—just a wall with niches for the urns and plaques to cover them—but Stephanie had questions about how it worked. Did we need a license? Was there a ceremony for placing the urn in the niche? How much did it cost? She was satisfied with the answers she received, and we made arrangements to deposit Walt's ashes there the following Saturday.

We were about to leave when I noticed Phyllis wasn't with us. We found her seated on a bench in the garden across from the church entrance. A stone wall separated the garden from the sidewalk. Engraved on it was a verse from Lamentations that read, "The steadfast love of the Lord never ceases, His mercies never come to an end."

"It's very peaceful here," she said as we came to sit beside her.

"Yes," I replied. "It is."

"I've never attended church."

The priest was still with us. "We have a service at eight o'clock on Sunday morning," he said. "You might like it. We sing one hymn. The rest of the liturgy is spoken. And the sermon is short. It's not a long service."

"I might try that sometime," Phyllis said. "But I like it out here."

"Come anytime," he replied. "And stay as long as you like."

And that's what Phyllis did. She went to the church every afternoon at two and sat on that bench, her hands resting on her lap, facing the wall with the scripture engraved on it. I never knew why she came at two, but she was there every day.

She died in her sleep a few months after that first visit to the church. I'm sure that as she breathed her last, and slipped away from this life, God was there to greet her for the next.

Eventually, the pandemic passed, and we learned not to worry about it so much. Stephanie had her baby. A girl, whom she named Constance Maureen. It sounded like an old name, but I was honored that she was named, at least in part, after me. Even now I cry when I think about it. Stephanie and I operated the company together, usually with Connie at our side. Most people who didn't know our story thought Stephanie was my daughter. I did nothing to change their minds. It would have been awkward to explain it and besides, it was no one's business but our own. They didn't need to know about all that went on between us.

On my eightieth birthday, we completed the final phase of the project Walt and I had dreamed of developing when we were young. That same day, I signed a document that gave Stephanie ownership of the business, and I retired for good. I always suspected Walt knew I would do that, and I often wondered if he hadn't arranged his will for that purpose. Maybe one day I'll see him and find out.

As for now, I spend most of my time working in the yard and visiting with Allison. She's not as young as she used to be, but she comes over every morning and we sit together at the kitchen table. It's different with Phyllis gone, but we remember her fondly and once in a while refer to her in conversation as if she were there. Allison thinks we shouldn't do that. I'm sure Phyllis doesn't mind being remembered.

A young couple bought Phyllis' house—Dave and Leslie from Dallas. He works in the oil business. She stays at home. They hope to start a family soon. Neither of them has ever attended church and Leslie doesn't drink coffee, but we learned she enjoys hot tea. I bought a pot like the ones they use in England and found a store in town that sells the tea Leslie enjoys most. We brew a pot each morning and she joins us. It's good to have neighbors and even better when you make them your friends.